BONFIRE

BONFIRE NIGHT

James Mitchell

severn
House

This first world edition published in Great Britain 2002 by
SEVERN HOUSE PUBLISHERS LTD of
9–15 High Street, Sutton, Surrey SM1 1DF.
This first world edition published in the USA 2002 by
SEVERN HOUSE PUBLISHERS INC of
595 Madison Avenue, New York, N.Y. 10022.

British Library Cataloguing in Publication Data

Mitchell, James, 1926-
    Bonfire night
    1.   Suspense fiction
    I.   Title
    823.9'14 [F]

    ISBN 0-7278-5878-5

Typeset by Palimpsest Book Production Ltd.,
Polmont, Stirlingshire, Scotland.
Printed and bound in Great Britain by
MPG Books Ltd., Bodmin, Cornwall.

Prologue

He should have worn a raincoat. The trouble was, when he'd left the hotel, the sun had been shining in the sneaky way it does in Northern Europe. All promise and no fulfilment, would it be? He'd have to look it up. That columnist in the paper. The one who thought the only way to solve the world's problems was to get in a rage and stay there. All for fulfilment, that one. Trouble was, if they went too far, blokes like Callan would be cleaning weapons, checking equipment, counting live ammo, dying. But not Callan.

Not any more. Major, Parachute Regiment (Retd.). That was him. Like a letter to *The Times* – the *Mirror* only wanted corporals. A breeze got up. It was southerly but it served him right for not concentrating . . . The Negev, now. You knew where you were in the Negev. Bloody hot. Just about ready to fry . . . But the heat was kind, that was the point. Like the picture of a blast furnace on a Get Well card. And he *had* got well. Healed up a treat. No pain even, not any more, once the skin grafts had healed. They'd done him proud. The rain fell harder.

But what now, Mr Struck-it-Rich, suite at the Connaught? Go to Bond Street and buy a raincoat? Phone that up West number? Rent-a-Bird? Half of bitter in the Jolly Swagman in Earl's Court and have a fight? Aussies always enjoyed a fight till you started hitting them seriously. Time to go home. Get on a bus and look at London and think about the movie he'd seen, how easy it all was when all you had to do was lie very still and remember not to blink . . .

A bus pulled in at the stop. Big. Red. Time to move, and move he did. Four yards to go when the conductor rang the bell and he came second. Served him right for wearing a Hackett

1

suit. Hackett suits were taxi fodder. And there was one. Ready and waiting, except there was a fat woman taking on all comers and holding a golf umbrella like an old-fashioned rifle and bayonet while what looked like seventeen kids swarmed in. Yomp, he thought. That's all there is left. At least he wasn't carrying a full pack. The rain fell harder still. Horrible as it was, he'd have to use the underpass to the tube. Grotty stairs, scaling handrails, graffiti either meaningless or nasty, trash for a carpet, every third light US. How did they do it? Bring tools, a ladder, pretend to be window cleaners? In an *underpass*? And there, oh boy, there they were. Tweedledum and Tweedledee, already bothered about who would get the Patek Philippe watch. He looked over his shoulder and there was number three. Little Jack Horner. Three fine, upstanding lads. Aged eighteen, say. Smart suits, shining shoes, but not Hackett, not Crockett and Jones. And they hated him because he had these things and they hadn't, and because he was old. (Anybody over thirty was old.) Then the knives appeared – heavy, no crossguard, butchers' equipment. Chefs'. Ah well, best get on with it.

He took off like a sprinter, running straight at them, and they were flummoxed. Of course they were. This wasn't in the manual at all. What he was supposed to do was burst into tears and beg for mercy. What he did was swerve like a rugby player, bundle Tweedledee into Tweedledum as their knives slashed empty air, then grab back Tweedledee, use his elbow on him, then twist his arm and throw him at the wall, where the graffiti said *Sod Man U*. There was a thin cracking sound and Tweedledee began to scream and he grabbed Tweedledum, threw him like a missile at Jack Horner and heard his wrist go . . . So did Jack, and he would have come in fast if Tweedledum hadn't been in the way, and he kicked him. Sad really. Crockett and Jones doing a Doc Martens' job, but the old man scored. Bang on target – and Jack made a noise like a whoopee cushion deflating, then he sort of slumped and made no noise at all . . .

The well-dressed man walked briskly to the exit, not running, then up the stairs, where – *Oh joy! Oh rapture!* – an empty cab waited just for him . . . The Connaught. He'd

2

had his fight. A largish Scotch and water at the bar, and then upstairs for a quiet night: a steak, a salad and a bottle of Gevrey Chambertin, and Sir Charles Oman for company. Only he really ought to phone Dr Rabin first. After all, he had promised. Rabin answered on the third ring, heard the words 'Leslie? Shalom,' sighed and said, 'I'm on my way.' The gefilte fish looked delicious and he said something nasty in Yiddish, then his wife said something even nastier in Hebrew.

'Three, you say?'

Callan nodded.

'And how long did it take?'

Callan shrugged. 'A couple of minutes, maybe two and a half . . .'

'David,' Rabin said, 'I know you wouldn't lie to me . . .'

'Why should I?' Callan said. 'It's quick because they want to be quick. Carve you up, nick your wallet, scarper. And I was quick because it's the best way to win . . . obviously . . . I won.'

'One dead?'

'Just the one,' said Callan. 'I broke another bloke's arm. Third was just a broken wrist. Maybe he was concussed an' all.'

'And you?'

'Not a scratch,' Callan said. 'Not even my suit. I checked.'

'I mean, did you help them?'

'Well, of course not,' Callan said. 'They'd been trying to kill me.'

'They could have just been trying to frighten you.'

Callan pictured them. Smart lads. Ambitious. On the threshold of life, as they say. Raincoats, all three, to sop up the blood, then throw them away when it was over.

'They wanted me dead, Leslie,' he said. 'Or somebody did. Brand new knives. Best quality. Sabatier. And the fee. Wouldn't be cheap, those lads. You better tell Avram.'

'I'll phone,' Rabin said, 'but that's not my job.'

'You sure?' Callan asked. 'I thought your job was keeping me alive.' Rabin sighed. This one had been in the Negev too long. He even argued like a Jew.

3

'Just one more question,' he said. Callan's eyes strayed to his book. Sir Charles Oman's *History of the Peninsular War*. It so often was. And beside it two half-finished model soldiers, a French cuirassier and a British rifleman.

'Do you need something to help you sleep?'

'A blonde would be nice,' said Callan.

What he got was Voss. Whenever he wanted to empty his mind, have room only for the trickle of water in a stream, birdsong, the green glint of trees on low and gentle hills, just as Dr Rabin had told him, in would stroll Oberleutnant Hermann Voss, jackboots gleaming, Zippo at the ready, the pride of the Stasi, and always the same greeting, *Guten Tag*, the most terrifying words Callan had ever heard. And none of your gentle hills and birdsong for Voss. A small, padded room, a claustrophobic room, and manacles and leg irons, and the only sound the screams of men and the click click click of the Zippo lighter: on off, on off, on off, till, light as a whisper, the flame touched your skin and the pain was unendurable, and yet it had to be endured – you were shackled so you couldn't move – and you too began to scream.

Not the brightest of men, Voss, though very possibly the cruellest, but then he didn't have to be bright. All he had to do was grill you like meat, until at last the questions came, and the commands. Tell me what you know about the CIA, M16 and the section you work for. Why was it always Hunter's section, no matter who was in charge? Why did you always use a Smith and Wesson .357? That man in the cell next to you. The Jew. Is his name really Avram? How much does he know? About Mossad? About the new Israeli tank? About the Israeli Army's last manoeuvres? And on and on and on until blisters covered your body.

Voss's snatch squad had lifted him in West Berlin. In those days, Berlin was two cities, East and West, side by side and a million miles apart. The good guys and the bad guys. He'd liked West Berlin. Promotion, good money, bad girls when he had time, until one of the girls had sold him to the Stasi. They'd promised her ten thousand Swiss francs but they'd killed her instead. Cheaper. But they wouldn't kill Callan, not even when he begged them to. Voss was having too much fun. And then the sun came out and it was the Negev and no sign of Voss, just doctors and nurses who fought like maniacs to save him. Maniacs. He did a bit in that line himself now. They'd saved most of the rest of him – new face, even new fingertips – but his sanity was past repair. Mad as a hatter, which was why he was poor old Rabin's patient. Wouldn't do to let him out on his own.

Mind you, he thought, maybe it's just as well I'm round the twist. Only a loony would tackle three fine upstanding lads tooled up with Sabatier carving knives, and him with only his hands and feet. He picked up the French soldier and a paintbrush and killed him with one dab. A bullet in his chest. Then – better make sure, he thought, and shot him in the head. What's the French for swaddy? he wondered.

And so, of course, the new Hunter wanted him back, which was ridiculous. Him being barmy. Unless that was the point. Like his mates in the underpass. Surplus to requirement. The old nutter might have just one more job left in him – like saving the skins of a bunch of randy young oil sheikhs, and if he got knocked off in the process, well, it sort of kept things tidy. All the Hunters he'd known liked things tidy. But this one had made a boo boo. He hadn't allowed for Roger Bullevant.

Roger. Oldest mate he had. In his naughty days, they'd gone thieving together. Best peterman he'd ever known. Open a safe like it was a back door with a Yale lock and he had the key. Only, he was the nervous type. Needed a minder. Hence his mate Callan. Those days he'd been the niffy type as well. First sign of trouble and he stank to high heaven. What was it that old judge had said? Had he fragrance, that was it. No he had not. Which was why they called him Lonely. But not any more. Now he really did have fragrance. Chanel's Allure for Men, and very nice too.

These days he had clout as well. Enormous clout. And all on account of the nick. Rehabilitation classes. Electronics. Roger found he could do to computers what he'd done to locks, and now he was a millionaire. Legit too. He even paid income tax. Not too much, though. Roger knew every bent accountant money could buy. He, Callan, had helped him out when he was skint. A small matter of fifty million quid. Roger had gone

5

on to multiply it by twenty times at least, but that was why his business was called BC Electronics plc. Bullevant Callan. Fifty million or fifty pence, Roger never forgot. Never.

They should have thought of that – whoever *they* were. HMG for one. Roger was daft about the Queen – die for her any day – but her collected ministers were high on his list of those to be thrown from the sleigh when the wolves closed in. And yet they'd spent a fortune supplying him with bodyguards. Sass's best. Not that Rog minded. They were nice and polite and he taught them a few tricks – thieving, cheating at cards. They got on fine. The trouble was, HMG expected him to pay for it. He'd done his nut. Even shown them his tax returns. And they'd left him alone. All the same, he'd lifted one of their wallets – taken the Sass lads out to lunch on the proceeds.

So they set the CIA on to watch him as well, but Rog didn't mind the CIA. Americans take it for granted they'll have to pay, being Americans, and one of them, Chuck, shared his enthusiasm for classic American cars. Even found him a Dusenberg. That was fine. Trouble was, he couldn't figure out why the CIA was in his flat all the time. Big, that flat. What they called a duplex. Gently, Callan had explained.

'First you got Sass, right?'

'Right,' said Roger.

'Now why did you get Sass?'

'Because they're the best,' said Roger.

Callan sighed. 'What I mean,' he said, 'why should the government give you free bodyguards?'

'Because I won't bleeding pay,' said Roger.

Gently, Callan told himself. Kindly. He's your mate.

'What I mean,' he said again, 'you must have something they want.'

Roger shot to his feet.

'Now look here, Dave,' he said. 'I was never like that. Never will be. Not even in the nick.'

'Well of course you—'

'Big birds is what I like,' Roger said. 'You know that . . .'

''Course I know,' said Callan. 'Only I'm not talk—'

6

'And anyway,' said Roger, 'you're supposed to be my mate. Some mate. Casting incinerations . . .'

'Belt up,' said Callan, and Roger took one look at him and did just that. Callan didn't even have to shout, just *be* there.

'You've got Sass because we work for the government, because we make stuff for them. Secret stuff that you designed. Everybody else wants it but the Queen's got it. Because of you.'

That went down well. The Queen and money.

'But the stuff you dream up – it's expensive. Costs a fortune.'

'We've got a fortune,' said Roger.

Keep going, thought Callan. Straight on.

'And very nice too,' he said. 'But we like our money up front, and sometimes HMG's a bit short of readies, so they—'

'Are you telling me I belong to the Yanks?'

'A piece of you. A piece of me, too,' said Callan, and waited for the sky to fall.

Her Majesty the Queen was one thing, Mr President quite another . . . Roger brooded.

'Yanks like Chuck?' he said at last.

'Likely,' Callan said.

'Ah well, that's different,' Roger said. 'Chuck's all right. I showed him my Agony portrait of the Queen.'

'Annigoni,' said Callan.

'I'm not with you, Dave.'

'The painter,' said Callan. 'His name's Annigoni.'

'I dare say,' Roger said. 'All the same, if the Yanks is paying, I reckon we should put our prices up.'

Probably got that from one of his computers. The accountant, most likely. What was her name? Rosie? The one that spoke German. Which brings us to Naomi Klein, he thought. A bit slimline for Roger's taste, but definitely his bird. Naomi Klein MA (Cantab.), barrister-at-law, Roedean and Newnham, childhood home a mill house in Sussex, current address a flat in Islington when it wasn't Roger's flat in Grosvenor Place. Roger's flat. Roger's little Jewish bit on the side. And very nice too – except that it didn't make sense. Good looker, sure,

7

but the wrong sort of good looks. Slim elegance, that was our Naomi. True, her voice was pleasant. Low-pitched home counties, not too refined, but all the time asking questions. True, she was a barrister, promising junior, soon to be a QC, but even so – she went on like she was writing your biography. And on. And on . . .

She had represented Roger in his farewell appearance at court (larceny of goods, value one hundred and eighty-seven pounds thirty-eight pence, seventeen other offences to be taken into consideration), and had got him off with a suspended sentence, which meant she was good all right, but the next thing was one nobody was set for. She was swearing undying love. For Roger. It was ridiculous.

True, he was a genius, but he was also an ex tea leaf who didn't know his chicken marengo from his tartare sauce. He'd sooner have fish and chips anyway, served by a fat film star with a narrow waist.

Trouble was, he'd been away when it happened – Voss's guest at the Potsdam Hilton – and Roger needed help. All he could get, and he'd got the best, courtesy of some charity for the support of ageing villains who were hopeless and helpless. One Callan had never heard of.

And after it was all over, she stayed on, legal adviser to BC Electronics plc. Good at it an' all, and much fancied by the SAS and the CIA, but she was true to her Roger, like she was under orders, and now we're getting warm, thought Callan. She was a plant. Had to be. A Jewish plant. Not a sabra. He'd met a few of them in the Negev, and they were wild, no messing. Mossad's best. No Roedean and Cambridge. Nothing like that. Desert cactus, thorns like stilettos, though the blossom was something else, but the blossom only unfurled after work, and the work was combat. Gun, knife, hands, and Callan was number one pin-up because he was even better at it than they were. But not Ms Naomi Klein MA (Cantab.).

Better talk it over with Gerald. Camp as a Boy Scouts' outing was Gerald, but he knew his stuff. They'd brought him back into M16 after the Potsdam business. Coordinator. Hunter's Section, needed a bit of coordinating after Potsdam. Their German operator had lifted Hunter having a triple bypass.

8

And Hunter's boss, Bishop – in deep cover as usual. And then word from an electronics lab in Cambridge that there was a genius on the loose. They knew he was a genius, because they'd logged on to him doing things it was impossible to do, and yet he was doing them. And so it was Hunt the Genius time, and, 'Your country needs you, Mr Bullevant,' and, 'Send for the SAS . . .' *And* the CIA. Happy days.

They took lunch at Gerald's favourite bistro, Gay Gordon's (The Gay Hussar's gone right off the boil – all those meaty politicians) and talked of Potsdam and the CIA and the Negev chorus line and Naomi Klein.

Gerald knew at once that Callan was right. It was all too coincidental, too pat. She was Mossad. Had to be. All those questions and sharing bed and board with Roger. No doubt they'd intended to lift poor old Rog, but Sass had banjoed that, so Naomi began on the questions. It was what barristers were for. It was what Gerald was for, too. Prying, bribing, teasing for answers. *And* there was a rumour that Avram had been seen at Gatwick, and Avram was Mossad's devoted slave. Gerald sighed.

'More prying,' he said.

'Go on,' said Callan. 'You know you love it.'

'Yes, but it's a woman,' said Gerald. 'Lingerie drawer. Bras, knickers, bustier. All that. It's so – so unnatural.'

Sometimes it was difficult to tell whether Gerald was acting or not. Callan wondered whether Gerald had the same problem. He yawned. Too much thinking. Takes it out of a chap. Listen to the waterfall instead.

The Land Rover was old. Decrepit even. Paint scratched, side window cracked, springs long since gone to a happier place. Eight carefree drivers at least, and each one worse than the last: the oldest serving member of the Guardia Civil, thought Jimenez, and every year I'm ordered to drive it (no one in their right minds would volunteer), given Peña for a partner, and sent to guard a bonfire. And the comandante talks as if it was an honour. 'The biggest, highest bonfire in all Spain, here in Andalucia.'

And in a way the comandante was right. Tent and spirit stove, good food, good wine, all that, but then the comandante didn't have to spend time with Peña. Fat, stupid, know-it-all Peña, so fat he needed a shoehorn to put his pants on. It was – let's face it – embarrassing. A guardia should be lean, quick, hungry for action, running to meet it. Peña couldn't even trot. But his cousin was next in line for mayor . . .

Nice country, though, open yet somehow wild, and the high sierras glittering white, even in August. And the horses, and the bulls with that guileless look in their eyes. Do get out for a moment and I will teach you how to run even faster, Señor. And your fat friend . . . Thank you, Señor *Toro*, some other time.

And then they crested a hill, and there it was, a great tower of junk. Vast. Cars, workbenches, three-piece suites. One year, some idiots had added half a dozen worn out tellies. When the fire reached them, they heard it in Granada. Hence the stove and the tent and the stores. And yet, Jimenez hated this assignment – and not just Peña. That bastard junk heap looked like a figure. Not a man. A devil. It even had its offering of flowers all around it. Red flowers. Hot and glittering. Like blood. What names had the priest said, when he frightened little Jimenez, thirty years ago? Moloch? Baal? No, even worse. This was Satan – and Peña sulked. His turn to unload the stores. Peña could sulk for a month, never mind a week. Give him a sweetie.

'There could be people in that load of rubbish,' Jimenez said. 'Scavengers. Best give them a round or two.' Peña brightened at once, unholstered a Llama XV automatic while Jimenez moved behind him. Peña was a terrible shot, but his sister sometimes slept with a man in the Ministry of Justice who issued gun licences.

His first shot hit the bonfire smack on, splintering a chair leg that supported a sofa that supported a door, and the whole thing began to slide, and Jimenez prayed aloud, remembering again the year of the TV sets, and grabbed Peña's wrist and the Llama pointed at the sky, a big enough target but well out of range, and Peña continued to fire and out of the bonfire they came like ants from a corpse: drunks, junkies, down-and-outs, looking for something – anything – they could pawn, but the Llama cracked, and they moved like Olympic medallists

10

instead. Peña happily fired the last round, then reached for matches, a cigarette.

Jimenez knocked them from his hands, like switching channels on TV. 'It's a fire,' said Jimenez. 'Smoke . . . Flames . . . If it takes hold it will kill us – and so will the comandante.'

One

P eace, thought Callan. Calm. Tranquillity. And the sun like a blow, but the heat didn't hurt. Not here. The heat made you calm, relaxed, oblivious. Egyptian PT. Sometimes they still called it that in the Paras. Around him was bedlam, and that was like the Paras too. Choppers thumping, sergeants yelling, semi-automatics ripping through it all. Paddies and wogs and Argies, and he'd slept through even that, until it was his turn to kill them. Here it was the slop of water and kids yelling by the waterfall, and mothers squawking like a vulture's alarm cry. Calm as a cathedral's congregation.

The waterfall had been a cracking idea. Hotel Cascada. The only one on the coast. A magnet for the kids. Left you room to swim . . . He put his book down on his sunbed, walked to the pool and dived. He'd started to think of South Armagh when he'd been that second time and that wouldn't do. Better to swim till it went away, and even then those three young gits from the Shepherd's Bush underpass tried to take its place, but four more fast lengths and they buggered off, left him in peace, and then the waterfall, water like blows, smashing dirt like an enemy, the bugs and mud and sweat of a three-day patrol . . . He was clean till the next time: he could go back to his book.

Except that somebody else had had the same idea. Perched on the end of his sunbed, golden tan, bikini more cute than blatant, and her nose buried deep in Bullock's *Hitler and Stalin*. It didn't add up. Cautiously he reached for his towel and she looked up at once. Her face had a sort of clever prettiness: hair like dark gold, blue eyes wide and honest. Hard to believe that she and the three gits in the underpass belonged to the same species. The same planet even.

12

'Oh,' she said. 'I'm sorry.' She closed the book. 'It's just – it looked interesting.'

'Not to worry.' Good tan, too, he thought. Some young sprog was lucky.

She wiped the book, and put it back on the sunbed, looked up at him. For once, she didn't mind looking up at a man, and, indeed, he was worth a look. Dark tan, darker than hers, a lean and elegant body and a face about as responsive as a statue's. Ex boxer? But what boxer, retired or not, would read Allan Bullock?

'We did World War II in sixth form,' she said.

Gravely Callan said, 'My dad did it too.'

'We talked to people,' she said. 'Quite old people. So *strange*. I mean, it was ages ago – history really – and yet they still remembered. To them it was still real.'

Gravely still, Callan said, 'It was so big, you see.'

And then her mother turned up.

When he was no more than a lad, just a slip of a corporal, mothers usually did turn up at this point, but not like this mother. Black hair, pale skin, blue one-piece swimsuit, chaste and elegant; except it was wrong. Fire in the deep brown eyes, and every movement of her body said *Attack! Attack!* Just what have I done? he wondered. Her daughter's a dish, but not my dish. Now, Mummy . . .

'. . . that church,' she was saying. 'Saint whatsit. We signed up to see it.'

Her daughter looked at the boxing bibliophile. He was watching a bunch of kids in the children's pool – wondering which one he would drown first? – and she could see his back, which had the same mahogany glow as the rest of him, except for a pattern of fine white lines like thread.

'There's masses of time,' she said.

'No, there's not,' said her mother. 'We can't go like this, Ellie. We'll have to change.' She turned to Callan. 'I'm most awfully sorry Mr . . .'

Now there's a porky and a half, thought Callan, and aloud: 'Callan.' And then, doing his best to imitate her accent, 'It's Major, actually.'

She looked at him warily, and at last said, 'Jolly good.

13

But we really do have to go to that church, Major er –
er . . .'

'Callan . . . Off you go, then . . . Don't forget your prayers,
Mrs Rugg.'

Before her daughter's eyes, her mother stiffened as if the
major had jabbed her with a pointed stick, the rage poured
into her like beer into a pot as she turned on him.

'My name, as you bloody well know,' her mother said, 'is
Wilton – Fiona Wilton. Why don't you write it down?' She
turned on her daughter. 'And don't you start sniggering,' she
said. 'This is serious.'

Callan watched them go. The sun still burned, but it wasn't
a golden ball any more. Just the sun. Very softly he said, 'Oh
dear, oh dear, oh dear,' and went back to deciding which was
the nastier, Hitler or Stalin, but they dead-heated every time. All
he knew was taking them out would never have been easy, not
even for Two Para.

He closed his eyes – majors always think better with their
eyes closed – and opened them almost at once. Somebody up
close, watching. Mars, the fat one. Shorts, sandals, T-shirt. Gut
held well in. Looking down at him. Not to worry. With a gut
like that, he could hardly miss.

'Uncle David,' said Mars. 'I thought I might find you
here.'

Callan stood up, yawned and stretched. Nephew or not, you
were safer standing up.

'And you were right, nevvy,' Callan said. 'Come to see my
little home from home?'

'If it's no trouble,' said Mars.

'Trouble?' said Callan. 'Nasty stuff, trouble. Not for us.
We're the good guys.'

The car pulled up in front of the house. That didn't even begin
to tell it. A hundred thousand quid pulled up outside billions
and billions of pesetas. A Lagonda pulled up outside a sort of
mini palace, and not all that mini either, big and sprawling
and old, except for the electronic surveillance, the vast and
welcoming pool. And the car – one in a million, and this
amiable fruitcake had two of them.

14

'Like it?' said Callan.

'*Like?*' said Mars. 'I adore it.'

'But I thought you sold them,' Callan said.

'I sell Morgans,' said Mars. 'And very nice too. But that's the corps de ballet. This –' he stroked the Lagonda's paintwork – 'this is the prima ballerina. Pavlova, Fonteyn, Darcey Bussell. I wouldn't sell this for its weight in rubies.' Callan steered him towards the house before ecstasy destroyed him.

More ecstasy. A girl coming out of the pool, beautiful but never pretty, like the Lagonda, and – like the Lagonda – a body that was perfect. She wore bikini pants and no top and looked round, lazy in the heat, till she found it and put it on, called to Callan.

'David,' she said, 'I must speak with you.'

'Half an hour. In the War Room.'

'OK,' she said and wriggled, straightening up her bikini.

If there was a moon, I'd be howling at it, thought Mars. Aloud he said, 'Who on earth is that?'

'My housekeeper,' said Callan.

Mars thought, You can't win, so don't fight, but then Callan produced another one: a lean and handsome Spaniard, hand-made silk shirt and doeskin trousers – in that heat – who walked with a limp, and even the limp was elegant. He came up to the car.

'Shall I park her?' he asked.

'Drinks first, Angel,' said Callan, and looked at Mars. 'G & T?'

Mars nodded. 'In the War Room,' said Callan.

'Coming up,' Angel said, and limped away.

Mars watched him go. Hand-made boots, chain and bracelet of heavy gold, Cartier watch. Ten thousand quid's worth. At least.

'I suppose he's your butler?' he said.

'Just today,' said Callan. 'It's the regular chap's day off. Usually he's my pilot.'

'Pilot?' said Mars. 'You have a plane?'

'No,' said Callan. 'He has.'

The War Room was vast; dominated by a table equally vast; the terrain for war games. Stacked round it were hills, forests,

15

streams, and on it a battle. Troops in blue facing troops in grey, fences, cannon, the troops cheap models known as flats. Like the real ones, they were there to be shot at, so why make them pretty? Behind them was another table, splendid and somehow strong, and on it, superbly made models enacted the last stage of Waterloo as if it was a TV episode – no blood, no guts, no death, and brooding over it all the farmhouse, Hougoumont, its roof removed for repair.

'My God,' said Mars. 'This room's incredible.'

He turned to where a pattern of weapons – swords, bayonets, framed by muskets and rifles – glittered on one wall, its centrepiece an elegantly chased double-barrelled pistol, as Angel came in, followed by a man carrying the drinks. He looks just about finished, Mars thought, his handsome face as battered and lived in as his clothes. Angel took the tray and Callan looked at the man. That was all. He looked and the battered man vanished.

'Why on earth did you bring Bernardo?' Callan asked.

Angel said, 'He told me it is not . . . appropriate for me to be a waiter.'

'You're not a waiter,' said Callan. 'You're a mate.'

The elegant one grinned, and began to mix the drinks.

Callan turned to Mars. 'Angel is a torero – a bullfighter. Best in Spain, for my money, only—'

Angel interrupted. 'Second bull. At Salamanca. Hit my thigh muscle. Unimportant bull. Unimportant corrida, but he hit me. I killed him, but my thigh, my whole leg, I could hardly walk till your uncle brought me here. Phy–sio–therapy. *Un brujo* – your uncle.'

'Magician,' Callan explained, then shook his head. 'You're the one with the magic. Do you think my nephew could be a torero?'

Angel said at once, 'No. Not possibly. A picador perhaps, but not a torero.'

Callan sipped at his drink. 'Why not?'

'Too fat,' said Angel.

He raised his glass and limped from the room, and Callan went to the battle table, fiddled with a line of Confederate soldiers.

'Gettysburg,' he said. 'Second day. So far, Lee's doing fine.'

'Hunter said we're to go back now,' Mars said.

'Is that a fact?' said Callan, and moved a line of men in column,

'Pickett's division,' he said, and tapped the table. 'It's all up to them. If they can break Meade's line—'

'Look,' said Mars. 'I know I'm only the messenger, but at least hear the message. Come back *now*. At once, Hunter said.'

'I didn't,' said Callan, and Mars sighed. He hadn't a card in his hand worth playing. Callan picked up a model cannon, produced a pocket magnifying glass, then looked at a screw in the wheel.

Not a care in the world, thought Mars, then the housekeeper appeared, wearing what there was of a sundress, and Mars knew it was meant to embarrass him, but it made no difference. It *did* embarrass him.

'Please,' she said. 'I must ask you—'

Callan interrupted her. 'Carmencita – this is my nephew, John.'

'Nephew?'

'*Sobrino*,' said Callan.

'Truly?' Carmencita said, and examined him – as if I was a bloody horse, thought Mars.

'He's not like you,' she said. 'I think he sits down a lot. Young men should not sit down a lot.'

'Nor young women either,' said Callan. 'Get on with it.'

She took a deep breath, and Mars wondered how much more he could take.

'Next week,' Carmencita said. 'The fiesta. I've been asked to dance. Fifteen minutes. Not a second more. I swear it.'

'Let's see the leg,' said Callan.

Casually, as if he was a kind of overweight crutch, she held on to Mars and pulled up her skirt and Callan squatted beside her. Impersonal as a surgeon, he turned the joint, then prodded the calf and she yelled.

'You,' she said. 'You hurt me. You don't want me to dance.'

17

'Of course I do,' Callan said. 'And not just next week. For years and years. Just be patient.'

'For how long? It's been months.'

'Dance a few steps,' said Callan, and she did, and Mars had no doubt at all, even in seconds, how great her talent was.

'Soon,' he said. 'A month, I think. If you do as I say.' The hellcat vanished. It was an angel who smiled at him.

'Yes, David,' she said.

'At the fiesta – ten minutes. Then, next day, you rest. And the next. And then the weights again. Understand me?'

The angel was still in control. Carmencita cast down her eyes. 'Yes, David,' she said.

'You'll be sensational,' said Callan, and John Mars marvelled.

The best stick and carrot he'd seen in years.

'It's for your orphans?' Callan asked, and she nodded.

'The orphans always get the best.'

He grinned. 'I know,' he said, 'I'm an orphan myself.' And then, as if it was part of the same sentence. 'Do you think my nephew will ever be a dancer?'

'Of course not,' Carmencita said.

'Why not?'

She didn't even have to search for the English words.

'Too fat,' she said. 'Look,' and grabbed the roll of fat that covered Mars' ribs. '*Un gordo.*'

'What will he be?' said Callan, the uncle who cared.

'Business man, money,' said Carmencita. 'Lots and lots of money. In an office. And play golf on Sundays. It will be very boring.'

Mars walked away and looked at the Waterloo display. It was either that or start a fight he knew he'd lose.

'You go to the fiesta?' Carmencita asked.

'No one to go with.'

'But of course you have,' Carmencita said. 'Your lady with the brown eyes. At the hotel. *Una guapa.*'

'Who told you about her?'

'Everybody sees you,' Carmencita said. 'Talk talk talk. So close. I will dance for you specially. And then no more talk.

18

Make her happy. Old people can do that. It just takes longer. But maybe that is good too, eh, David?'

She turned to leave and Callan smacked her bottom and she yelled.

'You are a very rude orphan,' she said.

'You did that on purpose,' said Mars.

'I asked questions and they answered,' said Callan.

'El gordo,' said Mars. 'What the hell does that mean?'

'The fat one,' said Callan. 'Fatty.' Mars's fists clenched.

'Don't be silly,' said Callan. 'Come with me and learn something.'

He led Mars to a room with its door ajar. From inside came a rumbling sound. Mars looked in. The room was painted white. No furniture, except for a couple of benches, and on the floor a box-like contraption with heavy iron wheels. The box too looked heavy. At one end was a crude mock-up of a bull's head, but its horns were real. Angel faced it with a practice cape and dummy sword, and Carmencita faced him. Angel approached the bull sideways on and slowly, one foot at a time, advanced as Carmencita waited, as serious as he was. No giggles. No girlish laughter, until Angel called, 'Ah—ha! Toro! Toro!'

Suddenly the bull took off as Carmencita pushed with all her strength, and again Mars heard the rumbling sound as the horns reached out for Angel, and Angel swayed out of their path, the sharp gleaming horns inches away.

Callan touched Mars's arm and they left.

'If he was fat, he'd be dead,' said Callan, and Mars, still lost in the sight of such crazy courage, exploded.

'All right,' he said. 'All *right*. So I'm fired.'

Callan said mildly, 'I said you're fat, not fired. You're on the team. As a matter of fact, you *are* the team. So shed some weight, son. Fat bulls are the ones who lose.' He yawned.

'Couple of days and we'll fly to London, first slot we can get.'

Again the yawn. 'All this gadding about. It's not good for me at my age.'

To Mars's certain knowledge, he'd travelled two miles, and that had been in a Lagonda.

19

Two

Ellie had walked. She could have hired something antique – one of Don Quixote's cast-offs, say – but she liked walking, almost as much as she hated her husband, so she walked. And when I'm sitting down with a long cold drink, I'll try to figure out what the hell I'm talking about, she thought.

David Callan would know. He'd lie there in the sun while the teutonic ranting went on and on, and when he'd had enough, he'd just put his book down and snap her husband like a twig. Girls couldn't do that. They hadn't the build for it. Other things, yes, but not snapping teutons. That was Mum's major's department. She could almost hear the snap, and Mum saying, 'Darling, that was marvellous. Could you do it again?'

Because Mum did know the major, no question. She'd told her. In the Funny House, she said. The Laughing Academy. And yet, he didn't look mad. But that was all on the surface. Watch closely and he was far more crazy than Mum had ever been, hence the sound of snapping twigs . . . Oh please, Major darling. Can't you snap just one of them for me?

Too late. Hermann the German was already there. Prompt to the minute, looking at his watch, which meant they plunged straight into a row. An old family custom. If only he didn't look the way he did. Young and fit and with a kind of innocence which was all a lie. He was about as innocent as the Marquis de Sade.

'Spying on you?' he was saying. 'Me? How could I?'

'With those things,' she nodded at his binoculars – 'everybody knows there's someone watching.'

'Birdwatching,' he said. 'My bird.'

He's going to be witty, she thought. We can't have that. Back to the row.

'The money, please,' she said.

'You want me to give you money?'

'The money you stole.'

'But we are married,' said Voss. 'What's yours is mine.'
And he actually waited for her to laugh.

Oh, Major, she thought. Where are you now that I need
you?

She tried again.

'Maybe in the SGB, was it? The Stasi? That second-hand
Gestapo you make such a fuss about – you were allowed to
steal from women. Not here. My money, please.'

For a moment, rage made him silent. At last he said, 'You
would take money from a refugee?'

Behind them, the refugee's car was parked. A Mercedes
250.

Ellie said, 'I'm taking money from a liar and I can prove
it. I'm divorcing you too.'

'Oh dear,' said Voss. 'Such grief for me.'

'Like you've no idea,' Ellie said. 'The papers will love it.
The beatings, the kicks, the laughter when I screamed. And
not just England. France, Italy, Germany, Spain.'

Relaxed still, Voss said, 'Why should they care?'

Time to thump him.

'Fifty years since Hitler died and there's still one Nazi sadist
left – when he isn't being a KGB sadist. And maybe there's
more of you. The papers will soon find out. Of course they
will. It's the story of the year.' She held out her hand. 'So give
me my money. *Now.*'

Slowly, reluctantly, Voss paid out money. Twice he hesi-
tated, but she said, 'More,' and he went on paying, and if
he dragged it out, he was still losing and that was good. He
stopped only when there was no more money.

'No divorce. No newspapers,' he said. 'I forbid it.'

'*Jawohl, Herr Reichstandart,*' she said, and he drew back
his fist and she hit him with a handbag stuffed with hundred
dollar bills. A useless, ineffective blow, Ellie thought, but
then he stumbled, tripped and fell against the Mercedes, got
in and drove straight at her, but she leaped out of the way
and the Merc did nothing but scratch its paintwork on a rocky

21

outcrop . . . A really marvellous day, she thought. The kind you dreamed of.

She walked down the road, which was no more than a path with hopes for the future, and there was another car, but not a Mercedes. An Escort that should have been home with its feet up, the age it was, and a driver far too well dressed for the car. Hired, she thought. The only one left, and having one of its dizzy spells, but its driver worked on the engine and it sort of groaned.

The driver lowered the bonnet, saw her and put his finger to his lips.

English . . . Staying at the hotel . . . On a diet, poor chap. Not that he didn't need one, but not on his hols, surely?

He reached for the starter and the engine boomed like a bomb, then started, and he waved to her.

'Fancy a lift?' he asked.

A Cessna, Mars thought, one of the big ones. Club armchairs, Goya prints of a bullfight, a bull's head above the bar. But no dancing girls. If you wanted a drink, you had to pour it yourself, so he did, and just in time remembered to take designer water. Callan was watching. Callan was always watching, he thought. That's why he's alive.

Music. Flamenco, and the sound of dancing feet like Carmencita's, but it was Ellie he could see. Boy meets girl then buggers off to London. Charming. He turned to Callan.

'I almost forgot to mention it,' he said. 'You'll be frisked. You don't mind?'

'If I wasn't, I'd be worried sick,' said Callan.

The music changed. Gentler, more feminine. Ellie. 'D' you think we'll be back for the fiesta?' he asked, and when Callan nodded, said, 'They say it'll be good. Why don't you go? Have fun . . . Show off that car of yours.'

Callan said, 'It's all a bit complicated. You taking Ellie?'

Mars nodded in his turn.

'You don't look like it's your birthday. Why not? She's a little cracker.'

'Like her mum,' said Mars. 'But, unlike her mum, she

thinks. I don't mean Fiona can't think. It's just – she doesn't have to.'

'I know what you mean,' said Callan.

'But Ellie,' Mars said. 'She thinks all the time, I mean *really* thinks. Went to Cambridge. All that.'

'But so did you,' said Callan.

Mars shook his head. 'I went to Oxford,' he said. 'Didn't have to think for three whole years. And after that, the Army.'

'Ah,' said Callan, and that said it all.

'But Ellie went to Cambridge because she *wanted* to think,' said Mars. 'All day, every day. Apart from everything else, it's exhausting.'

'What did you expect her to do?' said Callan. 'Play rugger?'

'Just listen,' said Mars. 'Please. Even my business—'

'I thought selling Morgans was just a cover,' said Callan.

'It's a cover that makes money. You should hear her.'

'"What's the point of selling old bangers?" she said. "A Morgan! An old *banger!*"

'Then the sums . . . If a Morgan sells for twenty-five thousand, who really benefits? The banks? The treasury? How does it affect the price of bullocks in Bangladesh? Even when we—'

'Blimey, that was quick,' said Callan.

'—when we dance. Look at the moon. "How long would it take a Morgan to get there?"' He sighed and the water slopped in his glass. 'I fancy her like mad. And anyway, Hunter says be nice to her. *Nice*. What the hell am I going to do?'

'Take her for a ride in a Morgan,' said Callan.

Angel put the Cessna down no trouble at all, then, like every other Spaniard with a bit of clout, left it for somebody else to take care of. Callan grinned. How many bulls to pay for that? But Angel didn't even look back. Mars started to worry again.

'You've got the keys?' Callan asked, and Angel smiled. 'Enjoy yourself.'

'Of course,' said Angel, and carried his bag to where a

23

girl in a Jaguar was waiting. The passport clerk waved him through.

'I bet she's not there to teach him cost analysis,' said Mars, then: 'Excuse the question.'

'Maybe,' said Callan, and Mars sighed once more. Be nice to him, Hunter had said. How do you even begin to be nice to a gorilla worth millions?

'About the keys,' he said.

'My place,' Callan said. 'Eaton Square. He's fed up with the Savoy.'

'My God, he *is* rich,' said Mars.

'You can't beat the butchery business,' said Callan.

He produced a document marked OHMS and they were nodded through. Mars led Callan to a Rolls Royce, the chauffeur already waiting. A black chauffeur, big and beautiful and fit the way football players think they're fit, thought Callan.

The black man said: 'Good morning, gentlemen. My name is William. Your chauffeur for the day.'

William Wilberforce Fitzmaurice, thought Callan. His old mate Spencer's nephew. A bit chippy about the black and white lark, but some of it was real and some of it was expected and some of it he enjoyed. Just like Spence.

'Knock it off, William,' said Mars. 'This is David Callan.' He took Callan's case and his own to the car boot, and William registered shock and horror like an actor in a silent movie.

'Mr Mars, sir, please,' he said, 'I beg you, you mustn't do that, it's menial work. Black trash work.'

'Get on with it, then,' Callan said.

'Yes sir, Mr Callan sir,' said William and opened the rear door.

'You're not nervous being driven by a person of my colour?' he asked.

'Not yet,' said Callan, and William sort of shuddered then found his cool. And not before time, Callan thought. Spanish *liceo*, then Oxford, then Princeton and the Irish Guards. He should know how to control his temper after that lot.

The car moved off.

24

'So, you're in Hoxton now,' said Callan. 'They tell me it's lovely this time of year.'

'How can it be?' said William. 'It's full of blacks.'

Mars said wearily, 'Just drive, William.'

Callan used his officer voice.

'No, no,' he said. 'This is interesting. You mean, bones through their noses, chargrilled missionary for lunch – that sort of thing?'

William was furious, and it didn't help his driving. It was a long way to Hoxton . . .

Ellie dived into the pool and swam to her mother, lazy and relaxed on a sunbed.

'Such energy,' said Fiona.

'I can't bear doing nothing,' Ellie said.

Fiona stretched and yawned, more relaxed than ever.

'Do you think I don't know? You shot off for a walk as soon as we finished lunch . . . Did you see your husband, by any chance?'

'How on earth . . .' said Ellie.

'You were strung up so tight, Paganini could have played you,' said her mother. 'Not that I'd have let him. You certainly saw somebody.'

'It was fine,' Ellie said. 'I got some of our money back.'

'From Hermann? You certainly do know about economics,' her mother said. 'Anything else?'

'He asked me a lot about your major.'

Fiona said, 'Not mine. I – hope you were, whatsit? You know – discreet. The only thought in the major's head is to break your spouse into three parts. Like Gaul, would it be?'

Ellie said, 'I didn't tell him a damn thing, Mum, because I don't know a damn thing.'

'There's mummy's little treasure,' her mother said.

'I may not be six years old any more,' Ellie said, 'but you still know how to make me feel as if I am.'

The Roller might as well be a hearse, thought Callan. Gloom and padded leather. The mourners yearning for happiness and beginning to fear it didn't exist. Time for a laugh.

'Tell us a few jokes, William,' he said.

Silence.

'Sing us a song then.'

Not a hope.

'Do a dance.'

William might as well have been carved in stone.

Callan sighed. 'Have it your way. Pull in.'

This time William did as he was told.

'Now take your cap off.'

'What *is* this?' William said.

'*Do it.*'

For whatever reason, William did it.

'You want a fight, is that it? Here? Make Hunter's day? . . . You're not a house-slave now. No cap. No badge of—' He looked at Mars.

'Servitude,' said Mars.

'No chains,' said Callan.

William said, 'What am I, then?'

'One of three crooks off to peddle dope.'

'And I'm still the driver,' William said.

Callan shrugged. 'Suit yourself. But remember. Round here, if you're driving – it's your car, which makes you the boss.'

'And just how do you know that?' William asked.

'I used to live round here. Make it go, son.'

A smile flickered on William's face, flickered and died, but he did what Callan said and made it go.

Different address, same hopeless chaos, thought Callan. A scrapyard like a grave for what had once been somebody's pride and joy. William drove to a gatehouse, showed a pass and the gates swung wide. Strong, steel gates with electronic alarms, on through to a wasteland of cars, vans, trucks – rusting, useless, dead. Signs to add a bit of colour: *Hunter the Magician – I Make Wrecks Disappear*; *What the Heck, It's Just A Wreck*. One of the signs too was broken. Lording over it all was a massive piledriver. A bit out of date but still doing its stuff, by the look of it. Well maintained; brasswork gleaming.

A bell rang, and the piledriver smashed down with enormous

force on what had once been a coupé. In an instant, it was nothing. Nothing at all. Mars said, 'Time to go, Callan,' and as they walked away, the bell rang once more, the piledriver slammed.

'Man, that was beautiful,' said Callan.

They only went as far as the outer office, still grey, still nasty, still with no chance of a drink, and there Mars and William searched him, and found what they'd expected to find, which was nothing at all, and Callan looked at the piledriver. Then the phone rang, and the news was not good, not for his oppos, but what the hell – the sun was shining and his mate the pile-driver was still flattening all comers.

'Could we go next door?' Mars asked, but that was OK. The inner office too had a view of his mate.

They went, and just as well. The inner office seats had cushions, and a secretary, good-looking, austere, played a solo on a word processor.

'Why, Liz,' Callan said, 'how you've changed.'

'My name is Betty,' the secretary said.

'Liz sounds better,' said Callan, eager to help. 'More sexy. You should try it.'

'Don't tell me,' Betty said. 'You're Callan. Come in and sit down.' Then, to the others, 'You two gentlemen. The gym.'

'Mr Callan doesn't know,' said Mars.

Betty said, 'I won't tell him. The gym please.'

They went like lambs, and Callan looked out of the window. Up she goes, then the bell and a count of three, then bam, and nothing beneath it but a sort of sludge and bits that could be bits of anything, but far too late ever to find out what.

'What don't I know?' he said, and she shrugged. Nice.

Hunter was late. Hunter was often late. In the old days, it was just another way of softening him up. Now it didn't matter a monkey's what it was, except he had a lunch date with Roger.

'How about a large Scotch? Water? No ice?' he said. 'Is that too much to ask?'

'Get this into your head. I'm not a barmaid,' Betty said.

'You'd be a sensation,' said Callan. 'Especially if you carried a whip.'

27

For a moment she settled for a glower, then giggled, produced Scotch and water.

'What mob were you with?' Callan asked her.

'Still shows, does it? Light Infantry. And you?'

'Second Para.'

'My mother warned me there'd be men like you,' she said, and poured two large ones . . .

'Gutted,' said Hunter. 'Ratted. Crocked to the eyeballs. Out like a light.'

'At least she doesn't snore,' said Callan.

'Look,' Hunter said, 'I don't know what you think you're playing at—'

'You should,' said Callan. '*You* sent for me.' And then the piledriver bell rang. Back to work, watch it fall.

'At least look at me,' she said. 'It's not a penance yet.'

And indeed it wasn't. Mature, but then so was Fiona, and competent. More than competent. She had to be. No nineteen-year-old bimbos need apply. Not for her job. The very first Ms Hunter. The boss.

'Mr Callan doesn't know.' Mars, that was. Not that he hadn't guessed. But why the secret? Throw him off balance?

Somebody else's idea, he thought. Ms Hunter would have more sense. Moaned a bit though.

'I don't run such a bad organization,' she said. 'Not nearly enough money or staff but usually I manage. One week to the next. Then you come in and wreck the lot in five minutes.'

'The cat was away,' said Callan.

'And, oh boy, did the mice play.'

'How dare you?' said Callan, enjoying every word.

'Well, maybe not that,' said Hunter. 'But her office. It's a shambles.'

'She was looking for her ashtray,' said Callan. 'She says you keep hiding it.'

'What on earth were you *doing*?' Hunter asked.

She was having a bit of a kip, he thought, and I was remembering. Daft. Plain daft. I live in Eaton Square and Andalucia, and I was remembering Shepherd's Bush underpass. Barmy. But then that's what I am . . . Three of them. Eighteen, say.

28

Bright, eager, fresh-faced lads, like me when I joined. Raring to go. Only one of them went. Once again the pile-driver smashed down. Better than the pictures.

'Callan,' said Hunter, 'will you please listen?'

'Sorry,' said Callan, 'I've just seen what I want for Christmas.'

Hunter sighed, and squared the red file on her desk.

'Like old times,' said Callan. 'Green for a possible, yellow for surveillance, red for an execution.'

'You remember our filing system, then?'

'I should,' Callan said. 'I was in and out of the red like a dodgy financier.'

He watched Mars and William on the TV screen, fighting in judo costume. William threw Mars, who did a clumsy breakfall.

'Oh dear, oh dear,' said Callan.

'They're that bad?' Hunter asked.

'That's just it. They're not,' he said. 'Properly taught, they could be good. What do they teach them at training school nowadays? Sleep therapy?'

'Always the same cry,' she said. 'Not enough money.'

'You could carve it on their tombstones,' said Callan.

In the gym, the fight continued, till at last the instructor blew a whistle and they stopped, wiped their faces with towels, while the instructor looked at them. Life was pain, it seemed, the gym was pain, and they were the biggest pain of all.

'A little out of condition, wouldn't you say, gentlemen? Been offered a part as Billy Bunter, Mr Mars? And you, Mr Fitzmaurice. Try to remember you're supposed to be fighting, not dancing on the telly . . . I hear Mr Callan's upstairs. You better pray he doesn't come down here for a spot of exercise. He'll eat you.'

The phone rang and he reached for it, said, 'Five minutes. Very good ma'am,' then hung up.

'Hunter wants to see you,' he said. 'God knows why.' His voice became a roar. 'Shower and change. At the double.'

'Well?' Hunter asked.

'Why ask me?' said Callan. 'I'm not in the fifth form at Saint Bonker's. I'm an old man, Hunter. A rich old man.'

'You could take those two with one hand.'

'The way they are now – sure. But I'm still old.'

'Suppose you weren't rich,' she said. 'Suppose you needed the money?'

'Mars on probation. William – I'd have to think.'

'Think, then,' she said. 'I've got no time at all. And the other business?'

Callan shrugged.

'You've got to do it.'

'Because of what it says in that file?' Callan nodded at the red splash on the white blotter. 'Come off it, Hunter. Look at the computer. David Callan's a clean-living bourgeois who never did a naughty in his life. But then, you know that. You're bluffing.'

'I'm desperate, Callan.'

Mood switch, he thought. Woman's trick. I've fallen for it for twenty years and I still do. He looked at the monitor. Mars and William showered, elegant – and knackered.

'Blimey, you must be,' he said, and dropped it. She was very close to despair and it was real.

'About the other job,' she said again.

'I'll need help,' he began, but she bounced back fast and hungry.

'We'll get you a locksmith.'

'Some gung-ho twiddler who'll yell for his lawyer as soon as he sees a rozzer? No thanks.'

'Lonely?' she said.

'There is no Lonely,' said Callan. 'Not any more.'

Dead? she wondered. Rio de Janeiro? Doing bird in the Cocos Islands?

'But I do know one bloke. Old mate. Roger Bullevant. The best there is – only, he's retired. If he does a comeback, it'll be to oblige me. I'm the only one. And watch it. He doesn't have to do this. He's rich too. That's the best I can do. If he says it's a goer, we'll move as soon as we get the architect's plans.'

'What architect's plans?'

'The ones you're going to get for us,' said Callan, and the

bell rang, Callan watched from the window as the piledriver slammed.

'Beautiful,' he said. 'The perfect way to kill somebody.'

'Kill?' said Hunter.

'Think about it,' Callan said. 'All you have to do is lay the geezer on the bed plate and give him a few slams. Nobody would know he'd ever existed. Beautiful.'

She shot up as if he'd stuck a pin in her. But why? he wondered. It made no sense.

'You *are* joking, I take it?' Hunter said.

She seemed worried, but then there was a tap at the door, Mars and William came in and she looked better at once. She was about to duff up a load of muscle that couldn't answer back. Being Hunter wasn't all grief.

She said to Callan, 'Remember what I told you. They've got a long way to go still. Explain to them why.'

Firm but not rough . . . He looked at her as if she was the stranger next to him on the tube.

I'd have got more response from a load of bricks, she thought.

William said, 'Is that official? You're going to be our coach?'

Callan snorted.

'Coach?' he said. 'You? Ring o' Roses for beginners?'

William stormed towards him, furious, and Callan hit him almost casually, but William went down hard.

'That's enough!' said Hunter, 'I mean it.'

Back in the infants' school, Callan thought, and Hunter said, 'I told you, Callan. We need him. We simply can't afford a replacement.'

'Is that what he is?' said Callan. 'A replacement? I thought he was supposed to be a man.'

He sprawled at ease as William reached for a chair to pull himself up. Mars offered a hand to help, but he struggled upright on his own.

'What's it to be, son?' said Callan. 'Stay here and be a replacement, or come with me and be a man?'

Somehow William straightened up, shoulders back.

'I'll come with you, you bastard,' he said.

31

Three

In the past, Lonely-now-Roger's flat had been a monument, even a shrine, to clutter: Mickey Mouse clocks, a German helmet with a hole in it, a Wolf Cub flag, naked-lady lamps, a fox's mask – stuff even a junk man wouldn't handle. A rag-and-bone man even. But in his Grosvenor Place flat, even the junk was classy: a college oar with the names of the crew, an ebony-and-ivory humidor, a glass-topped table to hold his butterflies, a 12-bore Callan had personally made harmless, and everywhere statuettes of animals, and, being rich, he could afford them. Roger Rich . . .

Callan looked at the print on one wall: Lady Butler, *Up Guards and at 'Em*. Not exactly Rembrandt, but she knew her uniforms.

'Like the print, Dave?' Roger asked. 'It's an original.'

Easy, Callan thought. Stay calm, stay cool. It could be a long night.

'Very nice,' he said. 'You into soldiers now?'

'Nah,' Roger said. 'That's your department. Only, we won that time, right? Not like bleeding football . . . Now, this bit of business we're doing.'

'If you don't mind, old son,' said Callan, 'I've got a call to make first.'

'Liberty Hall,' Roger said. 'Use the database room.'

'You're sure it's clean?'

Naomi Klein came in. Smart, elegant, Callan thought, and eyes like gimlets.

'Swept it meself,' said Roger. Callan left them to it.

'And since when have you been doing your own cleaning?' Naomi Klein asked.

'Not cleaning,' Roger said. 'Sweeping. We don't like bugs, Dave and me.'

'I take it you don't mean cockroaches.'

'No, ta very much,' said Roger. 'Dave and me had enough of them in the nick.'

Somebody answered first ring. They always did.

'Message for Tinkerbell,' said Callan, then, 'You heard, mush. Tinkerbell. It's a goer. Peter. Peter, you dozy git. Message ends.'

He slammed the phone down as Naomi Klein came in with a Scotch and water.

'Roger thought you might like this,' she said.

'How right he was.'

She watched as he drank.

'Do you think you could talk to me without a drink?' she asked. 'Dreary as I am?'

'You're not dreary at all,' Callan said. 'You're sensational.'

'Naomi Klein,' she said. 'Sensation.'

'It's the job, love. Nothing worse than thinking you've retired, then finding you haven't.'

She looked at him, grey eyes that told you nothing, and a body that was hard all over.

'I'll leave you to it, then.'

Already, he was punching in the number. On the desk was a little bronze statue of a hound: eager, handsome, alert. Callan wished *he* was.

Not the Savoy, Fiona thought, but not that ghastly Georgian hovel of Aunt Griselda's either. It would do, waterfall and all. Well, it had to. It was all she could afford. Very funny . . . She was in her slip, looking at dresses. She'd brought the three that appalled her least, and even they were awful. Once, she'd shopped at Jean Muir. Sod it, anyway. Not even a decent dress . . . The phone rang. Wrong number. With her luck, it had to be.

She picked it up. Silence. The shy type. Nobody in their right mind would want to hear her speak Spanish. Even so.

'*Digame*, or whatever it is,' she said.

'*Digame*'s exactly what it is,' said Callan.

She simply had to sit down and landed smack on a ghastly dress.

'Where are you?' she asked.

'London.'

'Wow,' she said. 'You tycoons do live. I bet it was a private plane.'

'It was a magic carpet, but it was going the wrong way.'

Watch it, she thought. He's a crafty sod, even if he is an absolute darling.

'I want to ask a favour,' he said.

'A favour, Mr Callan? What can a poor widow woman do for a tycoon with all those noughts after his name?'

'Mr Callan? What happened to David?'

'He flew off to London on his magic carpet. But if he's coming back . . .'

'Of course he's coming back.'

'Then tell me about the favour Fiona could do for David.'

She looked again at the dress. It really was awful.

Callan said, 'It isn't exactly a favour. More like a request.'

'David, you're killing me,' she said. '*What is it?*'

'You know there's a fiesta next week?'

Now we're getting there, she thought. Not that he's like that, bless him.

'The whole town knows.'

A deep breath. Goodness, how sweet.

'Will you go with me?' he said, and then, 'Hello?'

'Sorry. I was thinking,' she said. 'This fiesta thrash is couples only – goodness, how old-fashioned – and I'm only half a couple, so I thought I'd go to the Under-Nineties Olde Time Dance instead. They let singles in if they grovel. For the ladies' excuse me.'

'Fiona, for God's sake . . .' Callan said.

'I thought I might meet an enterprising under-ninety who would ply me with cocoa and Eccles cakes, and out of nowhere, you ask me to go to a place where there's wine and music and perhaps laughter too. Of course I'll go with you.'

34

'That's marvellous.'

'You know Ellie's going?' she said.

'With John,' said Callan. 'He got lucky too. But he didn't hit the jackpot. Like me.'

Warily, she said, 'Ellie will be my chaperone. She always is. She's awfully strict.'

'Not this time. John's new Morgan's arrived.'

'Ellie says it's a two-seater.'

'Not to worry. I'll find something.'

'Something splendid, oh lord of many noughts?'

'Cinderella's coach'll look like a skateboard.'

There was a chattering sound, then a bell rang. Even in Spain, it sounded technical and menacing.

'This is awful,' Callan said. 'I've got to go.'

'Work?'

'Disgusting, I know,' he said, 'but somebody's got to do it. Bye, love. I'll see you soon.'

'Work well, my dear.'

Fiona hung up, then looked at the heap of crumpled dresses. 'Oh, sod it,' she said.

Callan too put up his phone. In his free hand he held the little bronze statuette. He had squeezed it so hard his knuckles were white, his palm indented where the bronze had pressed.

'Have fun, Mr Mars?' he said. 'You just watch me.'

Ellie came in. Her mother was on the balcony: she lay on a sun lounger, but any drifting cloud would have done. Mum was away with the pixies. Shakespeare was the only answer.

'*She sat like patience on a monument.*'

Her mother blinked at her vaguely, as if she wasn't all that sure who Ellie was.

'My God, you look happy,' her daughter said. 'As soon as my back's turned.'

'For a start, I'm not going to the under-nineties rave up.'

'Oh goody!' her daughter said.

'I'm going to the fiesta instead.'

35

'I knew there was a feller,' said Ellie.

'Only, I haven't a single dress that doesn't look yuk. I'm afraid I'll have to accept your offer after all, darling.'

'Well, of course,' Ellie said. 'It's all my fault anyway.'

'Not all,' said Fiona. 'Your father did his share. More than his share . . . Where can we go?'

'There's a boutique off the Plaza de whatnot. Their stuff looks good.'

Fiona smiled.

'Oh super,' Ellie said. 'You look so . . . so . . .'

'So what?' her mother asked.

'Like you did when I was young.'

'And what do you think you are now?' Fiona asked.

'I mean, really young. Small.'

'Let's go inside and have a drink,' Fiona said. 'You're not small now.'

Their room, by holiday hotel standards, was vast. The bridal suite, maybe? Fiona went to the minibar.

'I must say those travel bods did us proud,' Ellie said. 'But then, we *are* proud.'

'The best in the house,' said her mother, 'believe it or not.'

A bit sharp. Maybe it was the G&T. Daddy had liked it rather a lot, and in Mum's book, chaps who hunted drank Scotch.

'Go on about us when you were little,' her mother said.

'Like when Nanny was away and you'd come and tuck me up and we'd sing.'

Fiona thought for a moment, then, 'Oh yes,' she said, and sang to the tune of 'Baa Baa Black Sheep': 'Ah vous dirai-je maman.'

'Not that one,' said Ellie. 'That was for when I was sad. Like that time when I'd pulled my dolly's leg off and Teddy wouldn't speak to me.'

Fiona put on her dress and said, 'Was that when you—'

'Hold on,' said Ellie. 'There's something I have to ask you first.'

'I knew it,' said Fiona. Just like a Victorian father. Mr Barrett or something . . . 'It's David Callan.'

'*David Callan?*'

Fiona said silkily, 'Ellie, my darling. You're my only child and I love you and all that. But watch it, my sweet. Just watch it.'

'No, no,' her daughter said. 'You've got it all wrong. I think it's marvellous. Just what you need. What you've always needed. Daddy never even knew where to start – but your feller—'

'You forget we met in – what did David call it – the laughing academy?'

Ellie grinned. 'We can't all have balconies in Verona.'

'You approve, then?'

'It's serious, isn't it? Not just—'

'A one-night stand?' said her mother. 'No, darling. It's serious and I'm serious and I hope to God he is too.'

'He was made for you, darling, and if he works hard, he may even deserve you. I mean, just look at you.'

She adjusted the mirror so that Fiona could see herself and she smiled and said, 'The song. I remember it,' and sang softly:

> Down by the station, early in the morning,
> See the little puffer trains, all in a row.
> Then the engine driver Turns his little handle,
> Chuffer chuffer whoo whoo, off we go!

Together they sang it again, louder, and this time they danced till the big finish, knee bent, arm outstretched, then somebody knocked on the wall next door and they put their fingers to their lips and danced to the door in silence, then tipped their non-existent straw boaters and sang fortissimo: 'Whoo Whoo, Off We Go!'

In the drawing room, Roger and Naomi sat, she reading the Law Reports, he a magazine so abstruse that only the masthead was printed. All the rest was diagrams. Callan joined them. In the nick it was the Beano, he thought, but that was before he knew what a mouse was.

'Get through all right, Dave?' Roger asked.

'Eventually,' said Callan.

Roger put down his magazine. 'That Cambridge . . .' he said, 'I thought they were supposed to be clever.'

Naomi Klein, sometime scholar of Newnham College, said to Callan, 'You look happy.'

'Well, so he should,' said Roger, and reached for a set of architect's plans. 'It's a doddle.'

Callan looked at him, awed.

'You spotted the cameras?' Roger asked.

'Took a while,' said Callan. 'I still haven't made the one in the spare room.'

'Crafty, that,' Roger said, began to unroll the plans, then let them go.

'You can see it better on the photos,' he said. 'Shan't be a tick.' He left them.

Naomi Klein said, 'I was his barrister. Legal Aid.'

'Yeah,' Callan said. 'He told me.'

'Well, of course he did,' said Naomi Klein. 'You're his mate.'

'For Gawd's sake,' said Callan. 'You're not jealous?'

'Let's stick to the subject,' she said.

'As your lordship pleases.'

Reluctantly, she smiled, then began to speak, fighting the words; no way to confront a friendly witness. 'Barrister,' she said. 'Lawyer. They didn't get a lawyer. Not that day. They got a cabaret act. Klein and her Magic Violin. Not a dry eye in the house.'

'At least you weren't topless,' Callan said.

'I'd have done even that to get him off. There was something about him. A sort of magic – even if he did stink to high heaven in those days.'

'I owe you for that,' Callan said.

But she scowled even at that. 'He needed you,' she said. 'Where were you?'

'Germany,' said Callan.

'Hardly Outer Mongolia, is it?'

'They wanted me to stay, even when I wanted to go. Wouldn't take no for an answer.'

She looked at him. No magic violin. Just brains.

'Where in Germany?' she asked.

38

'I plead not guilty and reserve my defence,' said Callan, and she apologized at once.

'It gets to be a habit,' she said, 'but Roger needed his old mate. Needed *you*. He got a Jewish mother instead.'

She finished her drink.

'When it was over, my computer went on the blink,' she said. 'He fixed it in about three minutes. It worked better than the day I bought it. Where on earth did he learn about computers?'

'The nick,' said Callan.

'*Prison*?' That one really got through.

'The Scrubs. Nothing dodgy. Practical Education Class. Trouble was, in three weeks he was instructing the instructor.'

'And you?' she asked.

'Bit of English Literature, because I like to read, and a bit of bookkeeping, because it's useful.'

'And Roger doing the rumba with ideas maybe a hundred other people on earth could tackle . . . So I dumped my husband – aren't you surprised . . . ?'

'Nothing Roger does surprises me,' Callan said.

'Exactly. So I chucked Humphrey out—'

'*Humphrey*?'

'Humphrey Nettles. He's a rotten lawyer. All he knows is bimbos. And horses. But never a winner.'

'Not like Roger,' Callan said, but she ignored it. A good brief could ignore Mount Everest, thought Callan. That's why they're rich.

'So I loaned him a few quid and he bought some second-hand computers,' she said.

'And the rest is history?'

'You know it is. We were doing all right – then Roger had this idea for a lap-top. Only it would cost millions – then, enter the fairy godfather.'

'I just happened to have a few millions at the time.'

'Roger says you agreed – what did he say?'

'On the nod,' said Callan. 'It's worked so far.'

'But not for anybody else.'

'He's the one I was banged up with.'

'So, for everybody else it's the charm.'

'Charm?' he said.

39

'Come off it,' she said. 'Working-class ex-soldier making his millions, and always with that manly smile. Of course charm. You could charm the knickers off a nun.'

As she spoke, Roger came in with an armful of blown-up glossies.

'Not E wing,' he said. 'None of those geezers fancied nuns.' He thought for a moment, then, 'No, I tell a lie,' he said. 'That religious maniac. The one with the funny tattoos. Revelations, they called him. Mind you, you could soon see why. Drop them as easy as God bless you.'

Callan looked at Ms Naomi Klein MA (Cantab.), barrister at law. One of a hundred, he thought. Gawd help the other ninety-nine. Then he turned to Roger. 'Come on, me old mate,' he said. 'Time for gainful employment.'

Four

Roger didn't much care for Broughton House, Marsden Square. Downmarket, he thought. No class. And, indeed, some vulgar person had tried to give it class when the class was already there, thought Callan. Now, Eaton Square – it was incredible, it was downright weird that he lived in Eaton Square in a house even a general couldn't afford, and all because of Zippos. But that was too high a price to pay, even for Eaton Square.

The two of them wore tracksuits with the logo *Hoxton Hunters*. Roger perched on a chair, eased a plaster rosette from the wall, the fitting for what could only be a phony Georgian light switch.

'Dave,' Roger said, and Callan looked up at last. 'You're not concentrating. 'Let's have the pliers. The titchy ones.' Callan rummaged in a sports bag and handed up the pliers.

'I owe this geezer a favour,' said Callan. 'So I'm lumbered. But you're not. Thanks, old son.'

'Any time,' said Roger, and unscrewed the rosette, took a tiny camcorder, then pulled a hair from his head, eased it into the camera and put it all back.

'Technical hitch,' he said, and Callan helped him down.

'You think the stuff's here?' he asked.

'Don't ask me why, Dave,' Roger said. 'I just got a feeling.'

'That'll do me,' said Callan.

The searched the room. Bed, wardrobe, chest, pictures. Callan looked at his watch.

'Maybe we better try next door,' he said.

Roger was on his knees, looking at the one section of floor that was parquet. Artistic, it was supposed to be, but it wasn't. It was a dead giveaway.

41

'Knife, please, Dave,' said Roger, and David Callan, labourer, handed it over.

There should be a sign, he thought. *Master Craftsman at Work.*

The knife had a thin, flexible blade, just right to lever up a block of the flooring. The incision, so to speak, Callan thought, and then the op: scissors, screwdriver, the pliers he'd already used, and Roger working with the kind of dedicated precision that reminded him of Voss, except that there was no pain, no screams, just a small and patient man doing what he did best. Not one of a hundred, not this time. He was the only one.

And, at last, 'Would this be it, Dave?'

Nine small, transparent envelopes and one large Manila-wrapped package. The little ones each contained a stamp.

'Bingo!' Callan said, and reached for one.

'Better let me, Dave,' Roger said.

Callan looked at him fondly. 'You're the guvnor,' he said.

Roger tugged gently at one of them. Wired. Well, of course, but the pliers took care of that, and Callan pocketed the envelopes, put the package in the sports bag.

'A bleeding marvel. That's what you are,' he said.

They moved into the corridor and suddenly a security man appeared like the demon king in the pantomime, but already Callan had reached out, and Roger knew there was just no sense in legging it.

'Evening all,' said William Wilberforce Fitzmaurice.

'We meet in the oddest places,' Callan said.

'Don't we, though? Don't forget our date.'

'As if I could.'

'Black tie, I believe,' said William, and then, 'Mustn't keep you. Jog off.'

Changed, showered, shaved, black tie. A couple of gents on the spree, and where did they end up? The section safe house up West. No wonder Roger was disgusted. *And* it looked like the waiting room of an unsuccessful dentist. Minders, too. William. Well, that was OK. Slowly, warily, he and William were learning to get along with each other. But the other one . . . Trainee. Here to learn and already acting like the headmaster. Then Hunter sent for Callan. More like a dentist's than ever, but Roger had Naomi with him. He would be safe.

As he left, his mate prowled the room looking for dust and the trainee began to get mad. It was his patch. Roger had known he was a copper as soon as he saw him. He tested the window ledge.

'Disgusting,' he said.

William settled in his chair for a little innocent fun.

'They're a scruffy lot, aren't they?' he said.

'Hardly the Ritz, I agree,' said Naomi Klein, 'but good help's frightfully hard to find these days.'

The trainee looked even more furious as Roger sprawled in a chair, put his feet up on another.

'No class, this place,' he said. 'No class at all. Worse than the bleeding Hilton.'

He reached out to a desk nearby. In a drawer was an empty bottle that should have held Scotch, and a plastic cup. He poured, and nothing happened.

'Stone me,' he said. 'Not a drop. Not so much as a sparrow's gargle.' He glared at the trainee. 'Feeling thirsty, were we?'

In her office, Hunter and Callan watched the show on the monitor.

'His lawyer?' she said.

'And live-in partner. She likes to be sure he's OK. And he can't design software in the nick.'

'And he's still good?'

'Still the best. Only he's retired.'

She tried to speak.

'He's rich, Hunter. The way lottery winners think they're rich.'

'If you were his minder?'

'Forget it,' Callan said. 'I'm rich too, I told you.'

'Too save your own skin – or your mate's?'

'You're a quick learner, Charlie. All the same, Burke and Hare would be better.'

'Bur— Oh, William and Mars.'

43

Callan went to the window. Traffic and lights and plastic shops.

'If I may ask,' she said, 'what is it about you and windows?'

'They show me a world that's more than Interrogation Room Five and a brick wall and a man called Voss, who's in love with a Zippo lighter.'

'Forgive the question, please,' Hunter said.

'No, no. It's OK,' said Callan. 'It was a wall that saved me. The Berlin Wall. Came tumbling down, as the song says. When Voss was on leave.'

'On leave?' said Hunter. '*Then*?'

'You're thinking again,' said Callan. 'I like it. Of course he wasn't on leave. He got word from somewhere and scarpered. Him and his darling Zippo. One more session, I'd have sung like Pavarotti, and yet he legged it.'

Once again, Callan looked at the London street. It was dreadful and he loved it.

'Left me to his assistant, Bauer. Good at his job, Lieutenant Bauer. Not in Voss's class. But he knew how to hurt. Like grilling meat for a kebab stall.'

Hunter winced. 'And then suddenly there were cheers and glass smashing and somebody yelling, *The Wall! The Wall's down. It's over.*'

He turned to her, his face wiped clean of emotion. 'I can still hear that glass go . . . Marvellous . . . You know, even now if I'm feeling rotten – like death – what I do is buy some glass and belt it with a hammer. Car windows are best . . . And then I feel great . . . Where was I?' He could have been talking about a film he'd seen.

She pitied him then – how could she not? – but behind the pity was fear. Overwhelming fear.

Her voice was a whisper.

'The Wall,' she said.

'Oh yeah, the Wall. Only, Bauer tried to stop me going.'

'What on earth did you do?'

'I killed him,' said Callan.

'But how could you?' she said. 'The state you were in.'

'I was crazy,' he said. 'You can do anything when you're crazy. Till somebody kills you.'

44

'If you don't mind my asking,' she said, 'who cured you?'

'Nobody,' he said. 'Some blokes tried – the best there are – but even they . . .'

He smiled at her the way angels smile, she thought.

'Don't panic,' he said. 'I can control it most of the time. Do you want me to finish this ripping yarn?'

She nodded.

'In the next cell was an Israeli. Code name, Avram.'

'Well, well,' Hunter said.

'They hadn't started on him – but they had plans. They told him. And anyway, he could hear me scream . . . We went down the corridor. The section head was there, stuffing hundred-dollar bills into a briefcase, and Avram killed him – it was his turn, so to speak. Anyway, I'd had my treat. I took care of the briefcase. God knows, I'd earned it.'

He yawned. 'We had their caps and jackets and a towel to cover my face – I looked like something in a horror movie – then we went and knocked-off a car. A VW. All the Mercs had gone.'

'Avram's a big wheel in Mossad, so we went to the Mossad safe house. There was a crowd in the way and Avram took our jackets and threw them out and then our caps. Threw them up in the air. Higher. Higher. And all the time he kept shouting, "Vrei! Vrei! . . . Free! Free!" And the crowd went wild. And that's what I did in the summer hols, miss.'

'Courtesy of that nice, kind Mr Bishop?'

'Smart girl,' Callan said.

'He's the smart one,' said Hunter. 'We don't even know what he looks like.'

'But he worked in the Section,' Callan said.

'He never went near the Section,' said Hunter. 'Phone calls, faxes, e-mails. That was Bishop. The Foreign Office had him in deep cover and they won't tell us a damn thing. Too many of the great and the good involved.' Hunter sighed. 'He and a Russian just like him. No more patriotism. Just money, money, money. The Friends of the Russian Mafia.'

'And Voss?'

'To Bishop he's just something you buy at the supermarket. Use the contents as directed, then get rid of the container.'

45

'Like that royal sniffer and snorter who needs help with his therapy?'

She nodded. 'Are you going to help us with his highness?'

'What choice have I got?' Callan said.

Hunter sighed her relief.

'So long as I'm the chief,' Callan said, 'I'll need a couple of Indians. John Mars is fine. William—'

'He doesn't like killing,' Hunter said.

'Who does? You're not there to like it. You're there to do it. Give him time. Handle him right, he'll be as good as his uncle.'

He looked at his watch.

'Time I was off,' he said. 'I've got to go and hurt somebody.'

The Consul Club meant more neon lights, but the arty kind, the discreet kind. The Consul Club was expensive, but Callan wasn't worried. He had far more money than the Consul Club, his dinner jacket was made in Savile Row, and his girl – well, if Lady Hamilton was a bimbo, so was Melanie; bimbo Premier League. And even if she still talked like a bimbo, her gentlemen thought it was cute, so long as her figure stayed like it was.

Roger and Naomi Klein came in. Roger waved and Naomi Klein frowned. But that was ridiculous. If Roger saw a mate, he waved. Reflex action.

'That's Roger Bullevant,' Melanie said.

'You've met?'

Her face said, *'Oh boy, if only—'* like it was there in print.

'There was a piece about him in the *Mirror*: "King of the Computers", "Fabulously rich". And a friend of mine told me the *Telegraph* said, "Minor genius", whatever that is.'

'He's all of that,' said Callan.

'And you're a mate of his. You must be fabulously rich an' all.'

'Just rich, love,' he said.

'How about hugely?'

Nosy, he thought, because it was part of the job, but nice with it. 'Cheeky,' he said, and she smiled. He was rich no messing.

William, now splendid in a dinner jacket, weaved his way through the dancers to join them. Melanie took one look and sat up very straight.

'*He*'s not a minor genius, love,' said Callan.

'He doesn't have to be,' she said. 'He's gorgeous.' William joined them.

'You've seen him?' he said, and Callan nodded. 'Want to say hello?'

'Couple of minutes,' said Callan, and turned to the girl. 'This is Melanie.'

'A pleasure,' William said. 'A real pleasure – your lucky night, David.'

Then he left them and Melanie said, 'You know all the good ones. Is he a mate too?'

Then her voice tailed away and she was silent.

'See a friend?' Callan asked, and then, 'Look at me,' and she obeyed. 'Now smile.' She smiled. 'There's a good girl. We don't want Smacker to think I'm a poof.'

'*You*?' she said, and then, far too late, 'Who's Smacker?'

Callan said, 'You're terrible, love. Just sit there and add a bit of tone and tell the truth.' He reached for the inevitable bottle in the bucket. 'You like this stuff?'

'Lager's what I like,' she said. 'Champagne's what the punters like.'

Callan signalled to a waiter. 'Pint or half?'

'Down the pub, I usually have a pint,' she said, 'but here they won't.'

The waiter came up.

'Pint of lager,' Callan said.

'I'm sorry, sir,' the waiter said. 'We don't—'

'Now,' said Callan, his voice calm, almost kind. '*Toute de suite, en seguida, schnell*. Get it?'

'House rules, I'm afraid, sir,' the waiter said.

'Otherwise, you and I will go out the back and have an in-depth discussion about how the customer is always right. And if you still can't see it, my large friend by the bar will take over and you won't like it . . . Think, my son. Ask yourself. Is it worth it? Intensive care, a broken leg, a mouthful of broken teeth. All for a pint of lager?'

47

The waiter looked at William. 'Any preference, sir?' he asked.

'Foster's,' said Melanie.

'A pint,' said Callan. 'Now trot along.'

The waiter trotted.

'Blimey,' Melanie said. 'You really do have clout.'

'More than Smacker,' he said, and she looked away at once.

Patiently, Callan said, 'I'm on your side. I got you a lager, remember? A pint.'

'Yes, I know,' she said, 'but—'

'You're worried about Prince Idris.'

She gasped aloud.

'Well don't be. His Highness is going to be fine.'

'Honest?'

This, her voice told him, is far too big a lager to be swallowed in one gulp.

'Cross my heart,' Callan said, and the pint arrived. 'Now you just sit here and enjoy the show.'

Melissa sat in solitary splendour. Issy Miyake dress of pink silk that had a sunset glow against her skin, ruby necklace, ruby earrings. Empress of Africa, she thought. Well, Watts County. Hunter was late. Not enough time to change. Gerald never gave you enough time to change. But then, he didn't have to. Gerald was the boss. Not just *her* boss. Hunter's boss. Still, this part of the club was nice. Thirties music and clumsy fatties who couldn't dance. And unattractive singles who couldn't dance either, but knew all about the wrong way to chat up a girl both pretty and black. Soon she'd have to smack one, and the management would be unhappy.

Then Charlie came in. Mannish suit in dark-blue pinstripe, hair in a pigtail, white silk blouse like a shirt, and Para tie. Poor darling. Melissa poured wine at once.

'I'll murder that bloody Gerald,' Charlie Hunter said. 'Why do I always have to be the dyke? What's happening?'

'Show's just about to start,' Melissa said.

Hunter lit a cigarette. A loose-leaf concoction from Cuba. Gerald was fussy about detail.

'Oh dear,' she said. 'Callan's got that *Let's all have fun* look.'

The two arrived together and William went at once to stand behind the target, and Callan looked down on him like a sample from a granite quarry.

'Wotcher, Smacker,' Callan said.

'Piss off,' said Smacker. 'I don't know you. You an' all, Sambo.'

William sighed, content. When Callan had first told him what they would do, it had sounded a bit much. Not any more.

Callan nodded to him and William's hands grasped Smacker's shoulders. Just another punter helping his mate to relax after early shift at the roulette wheel, till Callan nodded again and William found the nerve by the neck and pressed, and Smacker gasped.

Tall, still a bit of muscle, but balding, running to fat, yet still thinks he's tough. Let's find out. He pressed again: again the gasp.

'We're going to take you away from all this,' Callan said. 'Sit up straight when I'm talking.' William's hands moved, and at once Smacker was rigid as a guardsman.

'Now, where was I?' said Callan.

William said, 'I think you were going to tell him about our country club.'

'Club,' said Callan dreamily. 'So useful.'

Smacker had read a book once which told him *How to Succeed*. The secret of being a successful man was to dominate any group you were in. He looked at Callan. In all his life, he'd never felt less dominating. Still, he had to try. That book had set him back fifteen quid. 'See here,' he said. 'I don't know what your game is—'

'Of course you don't,' said Callan. 'That's why we're here.'

He looked at William, his hands no longer hurting. 'Feeling tired, are we?' he asked. 'Time for a little lie down?'

'No, no,' William said. 'Hands a little stiff, that's all.' He flexed them and put them back in place and Smacker yelped.

On the banquette, the two women watched. Hunter had black studs in her ears that looked like onyx, Melissa pink glasses Dali would have been proud of, receivers for the mike William carried.

'Well?' said Smacker. 'Are you going to stop this lark or do I call the cops?'

'Cops?' said Callan. 'Absolutely no need, old son. We've got a perfectly good cell reserved for you already. Lots of fresh air, healthy diet—'

'He could do with it,' said William. Smacker tried swearing, but William found a place under the jawline that made Smacker call out, very softly.

'You do that again and I'll yell the place down,' he said.

'No,' Callan said. 'You won't. Because, if you do, we'll take you outside and really hurt you.'

'Do they mean it?' Hunter asked.

'Callan does,' said Melissa, 'and it's William's chance to learn.'

'Is it awful?' Hunter asked.

'Ghastly,' said Melissa.

'A good hiding,' said Callan. 'You tell him.'

'There you are in that cell of yours. Austere, minimalist even, and in I come without so much as a by your leave – Sambo getting above himself, eh, Smacker? – and I give you a hiding you won't forget for a long, long time. But at last it's over, you think, but it isn't. I come back next day and give you another, and the day after that. Set your watch by it. And you yell your heart out, but that's OK, because a) Nobody else can hear us, and b) To me, you sound sweeter than Sinatra.'

Callan said, 'You really like hurting people, don't you?'

'Love it man. Love it,' said William. 'Of course, with me, it's pushers. With Smacky Boy, it's pretty girls who can't hit back.'

Callan shrugged. 'Takes all sorts,' he said.

'It doesn't take him,' William said. 'Let's just put him with the rest of the garbage.'

'You can't,' Callan said.

'My friend's just a big softy,' said William, 'but I'm not.'

'Tell him what's next,' Callan said, and mimed an addict using a hype.

'My friend Mr Softy's right,' William said. 'He's going to give you something nice. But in this wicked world, nothing's really nice.'

Smacker looked baffled.

'We're going to give you some naughty substances.'

'Don't bother,' Smacker said. 'I don't use it – and anyway, I got my own supplier.' He was almost contemptuous.

'When I say give,' said William, 'I don't mean in the hand. I mean in the arm.'

'I honesty don't use it,' said Smacker.

'You will,' Callan said. 'You'll love it.'

'Not the white stuff. Cocaine is for princes. But heroin's nice too,' said William. 'And every day, that kind Mr Callan comes along and gives you a bang in the arm that would flatten a hippo. You're on Cloud Nine, Smacks, and still climbing. No loneliness, no beatings, no reality . . . And then—'

'Ah, then . . .' said Callan. 'Poor Smacks – Let's go and gamble his money.'

'I'm barred,' said Smacker.

'Not tonight,' said William. 'This is your night. Let's double your money.'

All Edwardian, the gaming room, red plush and mahogany; and voices low and reverent. This was a temple, after all, to the twin Gods of triumph and despair.

In Epping, Mars listened, and kept his eye on the end house of the terrace across the street. Smacker's house. He'd crack soon, and there'd be time to drive to a pub that wasn't called something ghastly like the Friar and Boiler after the job was done . . .

'—We do something awful,' William continued. 'We stop your heroin.'

'Go back to the good-hiding therapy,' said Callan.

'But we're nice, really,' said William. 'All this knocking you about. It's exhausting. But it's not all bad. By no means. Because, one fine day, you find you're off the stuff. No

51

cravings. Nothing. You've done cold turkey. It's party time.'
Cautiously, Smacker relaxed.

'Except it cannot be,' William said. 'No happy endings for a naughty boy like you. A nice clean drug-free Smacker? Definitely not. And so we—'

'Inject you again,' said Callan. 'Back on smack. Top of your hit parade.'

'But you can't,' Smacker said. 'You can't.'

He was shaking, a rapid, uncontrollable frenzy, like the prelude to a fit.

'Of course we can,' said William. 'We're the bulldog breed, after all.'

'Why can't we?' said Callan.

'Nobody ever kicked heroin twice,' Smacker said.

'D' you know, he's right,' said William, and bet with Smacker's chips and won.

'If he's an addict, he's useless,' said Callan. 'I mean, we can't start thumping him again. It's boring.'

'What then?'

'Get rid of him,' said Callan. 'He's biodegradable anyway.'

'King's Cross?'

'The very place,' Callan said. 'Cardboard semi.'

'No money, of course,' said William. 'And that Rolex'll have to go.'

'He'll need some kind of watch,' said Callan. 'He'll have appointments with his pusher. All that. How about a Mickey Mouse watch down the market? Lucky Smacker. I've wanted one since I was seven years old.'

'Can't you just see him? All rags and tat? Got any change for a cup of tea? God bless you, guv. Foraging for fag ends.'

'I'm looking forward to it,' Callan said.

'Please,' said Smacker. 'Please.' He'd started to shake again. None of them was surprised.

Still on the banquette, Melissa listened hard and watched the three men in the gaming room in a huge mirror angled to it. Please don't let me feel sorry for him, she thought. Beside her, Hunter gulped down her drink and signalled for refills.

'My God,' she said. 'I've heard of good guy and bad

52

guy, but this is bad guy and worse guy. You're sure they mean it?'

'David certainly,' said Melissa. 'William probably. I mean, look what they've done already.' Hunter shuddered.

'You said there's another way,' said Callan. 'The trouble is, I don't like him.' William turned from the roulette wheel and scowled.

'And I can't stand him,' he said. Neatly, he stacked the chips Smacker had won and Smacker reached for them. At once Callan's hand came down like a hammer, the hard edge of the chips bit into his palm, and Smacker yelped.

'Keep your thieving hands off my money,' said Callan, and to William, 'Cash us in.'

William, lucky punter, took the chips to the cashier.

'Last Chance Saloon,' said Callan. 'That's what this is. You got a minicab account?'

Smacker nodded. He daren't risk speech.

'Use it,' said Callan. 'Go home. Pack a bag. Scarper. You've got thirty minutes.'

'For what?' said Smacker. 'Please tell me. I have to know. Please.'

'To vanish,' said Callan. 'Thirty minutes . . . Then we come looking. First one to find you – there's a reward. A grand. But not dead or alive. Just dead.'

Smacker sat there like a lump of wet clay. Soon he'd start the quivering again.

'If I was you, I'd leg it,' Callan said. 'There's two minutes gone already.' Smacker vanished like smoke, and William came back with money. Large, interesting notes.

'Very nice,' said Callan. 'Down the middle?' William began counting.

'My God, he's nasty,' he said.

'You'll see worse,' said Callan. 'Believe me.' He riffled the money through his fingers. 'Give John a bell,' he said. 'And congratters, dear boy. You did a nice smooth job.'

Callan went back to Melanie and found she'd acquired a mate. Roger. Each of them with a goblet of lager like a home for goldfish. Beside them was Naomi, pecking at a Martini, spreading gloom. 'Mind you, there's always the White Horse,' Melanie said.

'Out Bermondsey way?' said Roger.

'Do you a lovely sarnie, the White Horse,' Melanie said.

'Trouble is, they don't do Foster's,' said Roger.

'There's always something,' Naomi said. The thought seemed to cheer her.

'Oh, too true,' said Melanie. 'I remember—'

Naomi Klein looked at Callan. 'It's all too fascinating,' she said, 'but I rather think your friend would like a word.' She took Roger's hand. 'Fancy a knees-up, squire?'

Callan sat. 'This won't take long,' he said.

At once she was afraid. 'Smacker?'

'He's not well, love,' said Callan. 'In fact, he's ill. Very ill. I reckon it's the life he's led. I told him to go somewhere quiet and rest.'

'D' you think he will?' she asked him.

'He'd better, love.'

Not a real villain, she thought. But hard all through. Do as you're told, Melanie girl. This one could eat you between two slices of bread.

'I get so scared,' she said.

'That's over,' he said. 'We're your minders now, and we're the best. Like that comic on the telly. *Have no fear, David's here.*'

She burst out laughing, and, as she laughed, she knew. It would be alright.

'Just one thing,' said Callan. 'Idris is coming here . . .'

'So, it's true?' she said.

'It is if I say so. Got it?'

'Yes, David.'

It wouldn't just be pointless to argue with this one. It would be madness.

'Only, it'll be rough for him. No snow in September. No whacky baccy . . . The Sultan's booked him into a clinic. My guess is, he'll need a bit of company. How d' you fancy a nurse's outfit for Christmas?'

William joined them before she could answer. The kid's glowing, he thought. Ready to fly. Naughty Mr Callan.

54

'I phoned John,' he said. 'Time we were off.'

He smiled at Melanie and was gone, leaving a neat little package on the table. Callan gestured, and she opened it, loving and slow and teasing like a stripper, then suddenly she tore and ripped at the package.

'Oh, my God,' she said. 'It's Asprey and Garrard.'

'Princes don't shop down the market,' he said.

It was a necklace. Diamonds and sapphires bigger than ball bearings, even the smallest. Melanie just sat there, staring – a pilgrim who had found the Holy Grail.

'Oh, I do like you,' she said at last.

'That's nice,' said Callan.

'Come back next week and I'll like you properly.'

Mars sat in the Morgan in the neat suburban street, sheepskin collar up, cap well down, and not just for cover. It was cold. He looked at his watch. Warm soon. Suddenly the windows of the end house glowed red, a tongue of flame licked the curtains. Mars dialled the number on his mobile, and a voice answered, a voice that had heard it all, and asked the one essential question.

'Fire, please,' said Mars.

Five

How nice to sit in the sunlight, she thought, wearing a dress from Manhattan Modes – and not a bad little dress either, especially in the places where it fitted. But not Jean Muir, not by any means. Still, it was new and cheerful, and she wished she was. But this was important. Maybe the most important thing she'd ever done – and she'd know at once. Of course she would. And – oh, dear God – what would she do if she was wrong?

Fiona spread newspaper on a bench. Wouldn't do to have chewing gum on one's bottom. Vintage Laurel and Hardy that would be. And there was another thing. She'd kissed forty goodbye, and not last week either. She couldn't be wrong. Could she?

Mars drove up in another of his Morgans. Her daughter's rival, she thought. Not that it bothered her. Strong and handsome, the Morgan, and yet – how to put it – subtly battered. Rather like its owner.

They were on the edge of the airport's private runway. Tarmac, and grass that had decided not to bother years ago, and a scatter of planes she'd never heard of, some of them broken – she could find no other word – and always and everywhere the smell of fuel oil. Other men brought flowers . . .

She smoothed down a page of *La Prensa* for him and Mars sat, doing his best to hide a yawn.

'Poor John,' she said. 'Why aren't you tucked up in London?'

'David found a job for me – a habit he's got. I flew in on the – what's it – the red eye.'

'William not with you?'

'He's going to see a friend.'

'Gorgeous, isn't she?' Fiona said.

'So is Ellie gorgeous,' said Mars. 'Like her mum.'

'I call that handsome,' she said. 'I really do. And you just off the red eye . . . And Angel?'

'Counting all your chickens?' said Mars. 'He's due in with David any minute. He's flying David back.'

'No girl?'

'There's always a girl,' said Mars. 'This one's in bed.'

'*What*?' Fiona's voice shrieked louder than a jet.

'Oh my God, I didn't mean *that*,' Mars said. 'She works at a club.'

A Cessna came in to land. Oh David, he thought. Get a move on. You owe me, comandante. It was the red eye.

Fiona was saying, 'I don't care where she sings. I don't care if she wiggles her ears. But don't expect my daughter to behave like that. I know she's a married woman, but before there's any nonsense, she'll have to be wooed. And if that's old-fashioned, so am I.'

Mars was on the ropes, but he still had one punch left.

'Chance would be a fine thing,' he said, and she looked at him, bewildered.

'At the moment, she's working on a piece for the *Economics Review*. If I want to woo, I have to wait till she's finished her shift. Yesterday it was something called hog belly futures. Not exactly *Romeo and Juliet*, is it?'

'Oh, my poor lamb,' said Fiona, and a white Mercedes coupé, chauffeur-driven, appeared from nowhere and waited.

'Melissa's car,' said Mars.

'Somehow, I don't think William has your problem,' said Fiona.

The Cessna taxied in and the stairway appeared. William and Angel came down together, laughing. Two of the nicest men, two utterly charming killers. William turned and Melissa joined him, her only luggage a tortoiseshell handbag.

'No immigration? No passports?' Fiona asked.

'David's a temporary diplomatic courier,' said Mars. 'Acting unpaid. William's his minder.'

'And Melissa?'

'EU representative. Don't ask me what it means, because

I don't know. Neither does she, but it doesn't bother her. Doesn't stop her talking, either.' He smiled at her and took off his coat. Time to join the others, and the Merc and the Morgan. Together they looked like an ad for something unbelievably expensive: Château Pétrus, say, or vintage Krug, or a ski lodge in Colorado. But before he could move, Callan appeared.

From her handbag Fiona took out a Hermès scarf, even more vintage than the Krug, and tied it round her head. Callan left the plane, a canvas bag slung on his shoulder like an army pack. He reached her, not quite running.

'I couldn't keep away,' Fiona said. 'Private planes indeed.'

Callan smiled and turned to Mars. 'Any problems?'

'Not one,' said Mars. 'It went like a house on fire.' Callan smiled.

'Mustn't keep you,' he said. Mars's turn to smile. Off to that hog farm where Ellie was, and how many Morgans it takes to plough a paddy field.

'Mind how you go in that taxi,' he said, and went off to join the beautiful people.

Callan led her to the exit. Round the corner was a car. A guardia civil sat on his motorbike and watched it. He could have watched it all day, she thought, and when Callan appeared, he sighed, started the bike and was gone, scowling as if a goddess had kissed him and left and would never return.

She looked at the taxi. Elegance. Power. Like a tiger. 'A Lagonda?' she said. 'That's your taxi?'

'It's your coach, Cinderella,' he said.

They sat and cautiously he kissed her cheek, pulled gently at the scarf. 'The last of the Sloane Rangers,' he said. 'Is that it?'

'I told you,' she said. 'I was happy then.'

Gently, he touched her cheek. 'You're too much, Fiona Wilton,' he said and turned the key.

The tiger didn't roar, it sort of hummed, as if it knew the roaring was for later.

So much to see. The sierras for a background, their peaks white, even in the heat, which grew stronger by the minute; and vineyards, olive groves, lemons, oranges, then grass where two young bulls played at combat, and even their play was deadly. Then horses. Palominos. White, golden, bay, and a stallion, like a golden sculpture, that was a bit of a show-off, but kept well clear of the bulls. 'Slow down, please,' she said, and when he did, looked at them as if Stubbs had painted them, till the stallion whinnied and they took off in their own private Derby, and never a jockey to be seen.

'Oh, how marvellous,' she said.

'You like horses?' he asked.

'I like those horses,' she said. 'What's next?'

More grassland, more fighting bulls, and the high sierras gleaming in the heat of summer; and then he pulled up to stare at the biggest, tallest stack of junk she'd ever seen, and near it a *pueblo blanco*, the white village of Andalucia.

'A junk heap?' she said. 'After those horses?'

He handed her binoculars from a side pocket. Through them she could see the junk in detail – a bed, a wardrobe, a three-piece suite, and, perched on top of it, the remains of a VW Beetle. Then another layer and another, the pinnacle fifty feet up. Maybe more.

'Look to your right,' he said. 'Four o'clock.'

She looked and there they were. Two guardia civils.

'Two coppers?' said Callan.

'Two coppers. They've both got whatsits – machine pistols.'

'That's my girl,' he said. 'It's not a junk pile, love. It's a bonfire. They're there to scare off the nutters. The fire's next month, not tonight. You'll love it.'

'We're only booked till next week,' she said.

'We won't let a little thing like that stop us.'

She turned to him. 'My dear,' she said, 'you know how I feel about you. You must. But please don't rush me. I *want* to be with you. It was absolute bliss when I found I could be, but I mustn't rush it. Not this time . . . That's why I ran away from you. In case I hurt you. I couldn't bear that.'

'You think I haven't been hurt before?' The words were bitter but the voice was gentle. 'And anyway, who's rushing you? I'm a nervous wreck myself.'

'Oh, darling,' she said, 'how marvellous . . .' and he waited for the mood swing. It always happened. Every time. But not this time.

'You know all about me,' she said.

Easy now. Tender. Light. 'Well, of course,' he said. 'We played silly buggers together at Dr Rabin's.'

'It was *not* silly buggers.' Her voice a sword now. Freshly sharpened.

Easy, lad. It's how *you* feel, after all.

'Right, as usual,' he said. 'It was the best time I've had in years.'

She moved closer; touched his cheek, as he had touched hers.

'Me too,' she said.

Ellie scowled at her notebook. She had all the facts and figures, it wasn't that. It was just so bloody difficult to crush them into two thousand words. And then Mum came in. My hair all over the place, Ellie thought, no make-up, and sweating in a *most* unladylike manner. Her mother switched on the air-conditioning, looking as if she'd come to model a little Valentino number that Ellie wasn't quite ready for.

'Darling,' she said, reproach in both syllables.

'Yes, I know,' her daughter said. 'But this bit's tricky.' She was being defensive and there was no need to be defensive. She didn't even know what her crime was.

'You sitting there all scowls and scribble,' said her mother, 'and poor sweet John positively pining.'

'Dying of love, no doubt,' said Ellie. 'And what are you, Cupid or something?'

'Cupid was a chap,' her mother said. 'Anyway it just isn't *fair*. Poor darling John sighing all over the place and you sitting there writing about pigs telling fortunes. It's not *nice*.

'Pig's telling – oh, hog belly futures,' Ellie said. 'It's got nothing to do with – you've been with David,' she said, fighting back. It was the only way.

'Well, of course I have,' said her mother. 'In a Lagonda, would you believe!'

'Wow!' said Ellie, because fortune-telling pigs or no fortune-telling pigs, this was big stuff.

'*Wow* is right,' said her mother. 'We drove into the country and saw some bulls and the most divine horses, then a perfectly charming village. All geraniums and orange trees and roses round the door, and the village all painted white. Beautiful.'

'*Pueblo blanco*,' said Ellie.

'Very likely. It was called Aldente or something.'

'Come off it, Mum,' Ellie said.

'Well, definitely *Al*. We'll have to ask David.'

'And then what?' Ellie asked.

'He showed me the rubbish dump. Mind you, he *said* it was a bonfire.'

She smiled as if it had been the Taj Mahal.

'Oh, Ellie,' she said. 'The size of that country . . . The space . . . On and on. And all one – ranch, he called it. Like the cowboys.'

'How big is that?' Ellie asked.

'I expect it's all in centimetres – though, mind you, it sounds vast. Ten thousand – hectares, would it be? Sort of a farm.' She thought for a moment. 'But it can't be, can it? Ah well. So long as there's room for the horses.'

'Does he own a lot of it?'

'He owns all of it,' Fiona said.

'Mum,' said Ellie, 'that's twenty-five thousand acres.'

Fiona gasped. 'That's half of Spain. Must be. And to think we manage on six hundred and three.'

She looked at Ellie. Abstracted. Thinking hard.

'Now what?' she said.

Ellie said, 'Bulls and horses and a rubbish dump. On a date. He must be mad.'

'We both are,' Fiona said, and looked at Ellie, and smiled. It seemed the major had his methods, rubbish dumps or not. Her mother thought so.

'Never mind the rubbish dump,' she said. 'What about the roses?'

'A bit old-fashioned,' said Ellie.

'Well, so are we.'

'No wild passion, no gasps and moans, not even a heaving bosom?'

61

'In a Lagonda?' said Fiona. 'You'd have to be a contortionist, and old people like us have to take it slowly.'

Suddenly her mother looked shy. Ellie hadn't believed it possible.

'And I was nervous, darling,' she said. 'A couple of chaps after my come-out and then your father and that was it . . . The dull, the dim and the dreary . . . And then David. The most gorgeous demon king in the pantomime. Certainly I was nervous.'

'You're not going to chicken out?'

'Of course not,' said her mother. 'How many crazy majors will come running at my age? Raring to go – that's me.'

'When?' Ellie asked.

'Friday,' Fiona said. 'After the fiesta thingy. Back to his place. And, oh boy, will this bosom heave.'

In the hacienda gym it was work and more work. Mars and Callan fought it out on a dojo mat, judo style, and William stood waiting, in no hurry. I could give him twenty years and look at him, he thought. Snarling with the effort, Callan threw Mars, who limped away, and Callan beckoned to William, fast and deadly accurate in the game of high-speed chess that marks the good judoka, but Callan threw him too, then all but bowed, like an acrobat inviting applause. Mars thought: He's courting. He's got to be.

From her balcony, Fiona looked at a sky that seemed woven from a material she longed for and would never have. She was thinking again, but this time Dr Rabin wouldn't mind a bit. Not suicide. On the contrary. David . . . Getting her here. Getting Ellie here too. But Ellie must never know. She'd been so delighted. Good luck at last.

One of those clumsy, stiff and somehow unsympathetic magazines her daughter was so fond of. Competitions page – *Which mouse of the four illustrated below would best suit the BC Electronics Hammerhead Mark IX? Say why in twenty words or less*: and Ellie had written her eighteen words and sent off without delay, just as the coupon said, and bought a bottle of something fizzy when they won, and she, mum, in trouble again when all she had asked was why anyone should keep a mouse in a machine . . . No more computer jokes, Fiona . . . , But here they were, even so. They couldn't not be here, because David and that weird if splendid friend of his *owned* BC Electronics to the last microchip and they'd fixed the whole bloody swindle, and Ellie was the only competitor.

Chance of a Lifetime, the coupon said, but it was no chance at all. She couldn't *help* but win. They'd even had a special magazine printed. God alone could tell what it had cost, but David had money he hadn't even counted yet. She'd got it out of him in the Lagonda – even more money – and he'd owned up at once. 'But why?' she'd asked, and all he'd said was, 'You,' and what woman in or out of her mind could object to that? All the same, Ellie must never know, and he'd even said that first. What a man . . .

An imaginative man might call it a temple of death, but then an imaginative man would have no business there. A big bare room with adjustable lighting, everything from starlight to high noon, a table like the bar in a cowboy movie, and at the other end the icon, a blow-up print of the nastiest villain he'd ever seen, Nazi helmet and all. On the table, the guns: .357 Smith and Wesson magnums. Nothing fancy. This was to be target practice. Draw and fire. Over and over. And all three in lightweight suits, so that the holsters didn't show. Callan said, 'You know the drill. That man' – he nodded at the target – 'is the man you hate most in the entire world – just like he hates you.'

He picked up a magnum and at once it became an extension of his hand. Well of course it did, thought Mars. Years and years of mindless destruction.

'I'll show you just once more,' he said, and holstered the gun, stood with his back to the target. 'Call it, John.'

A silence so intense they could hear the cicadas chirrup outside, then Mars yelled, 'David! Behind you!' and Callan turned in a descending spin, drew the magnum as he went, drew and fired. Two red marks appeared on the photo print, head and heart. 'Questions?' Callan asked, but there were none. Mars shook his hand. William was silent.

'OK, John,' said Callan, and set up another target.

Mars waited, back to the villain, feet apart, his breathing slow and easy.

'John! Behind you!' Callan called, and Mars span and crouched the way the master had shown him, and fired twice.

This time the bullets were not dead centre, but either one of them would have killed.

Callan said, 'Hey, that's good. You get a prize for that.'

'Kiss the teacher?'

'You weren't that good. Go and phone Ellie. Woo, lad, woo!'

Mars grinned and left, Callan set up a fresh target, and William sighed. One of his long-suffering ones, thought Callan, with 'Swing Low Sweet Chariot' for an encore.

'I told you. I'm finished,' he said.

'You weren't finished when we did unarmed combat,' said Callan. 'But then, you're pretty good at unarmed combat – or you will be.' William moved in on him then – Good, Callan thought. When in doubt, go for the man – but, even so, his hand moved, and suddenly there was a gun in it. William froze and Callan turned it over in his hands, relaxed and easy.

'This is what we call in the trade a .357 magnum,' he said. 'Six-shot, three-and-a-half-inch barrel, weight forty-one ounces, nine inches overall. Front sight, Baughman quick draw, rear S & W Micrometer Click Sight, satin-blue finish, checkered walnut stock, maker's monogram. See for yourself.'

He lobbed the gun to William, who caught it easily, like a child's woolly toy, and checked it as Callan had done.

At last – 'It's an S & W, all right,' he said. 'Loaded too.'

The barrel swung in a tight arc, nosing at Callan like a hunting dog. The cicadas sounded louder than ever, and Callan yawned, but politely.

'No good unless you can fire it, as the young lady said.'

William sighed. 'No wonder I'm a nervous wreck,' he said. 'At Princeton all I had to do was juggle Athenian vases worth fifty grand apiece.'

'It doesn't show,' said Callan.

'Why the performance?' William asked.

'You tell me,' said Callan. 'Just say it.'

'With guns, I'm scared,' said William. 'I could cope in

64

the Guards – all pals together. But on my own . . . I shoot straight, but I'm slow. John could shoot me before I'd even pulled the gun.'

'And you could tear him apart.'

'I still might miss with the gun.'

'No,' said Callan. 'That's over. Let me show you . . . OK, you're scared. We're all scared. But we're proud too, because we're the best – and they don't come more proud than you.' He took William's hand, aimed the magnum at the bad guy.

'Now it's your turn,' he said, and William fired, a little red dot glowed like a cigarette tip on the bad guy's forehead.

'See what I mean?' said Callan.

William grinned and left, and Callan put up a new target. Six more bad guys. He picked up the magnum and fired in a smooth flowing blast of sound, right to left, then put the gun on the bench, took another and fired again, left to right. Each of the bad guys had been shot twice, head and heart.

He spoke in a posh voice, as posh as he could manage. Her husband – George, would it be?

'I say, I'm most awfully sorry, Voss, old chap. I appear to have killed you.'

Six

From outside her hotel room, the sound and flash of fireworks was like gunfire. El Alamein, say. Daddy had done rather well at El Alamein. Not like his daughter at all. Yet again she went through the contents of her wardrobe and Ellie came in and watched.

'Now what?' she said.

'I need a *dress*,' said her mother.

'But you just bought one,' Ellie said.

'And, like an idiot, I wore it. The same day. You can't possibly wear the same dress twice the same day. Not with the same chap.'

She looks at me as if I were talking Urdu, Fiona thought, but her tribe has its customs too, just like mine, and the Mad Major's definitely in my tribe. He knows all about pretty dresses – maybe too much. A rocket whistled and boomed. It could have been in the next room . . .

She pulled a dress from the wardrobe, held it up, then threw it away.

'Oh *bugger!*' she said.

Another, even bigger bang, and spangles of light like a star exploding, and then a tap at the door, a nervous little tap that said, *There's no hurry. Take your time. In fact, I'll go away if you like.* Already the hotel knew that Fiona had a temper.

Ellie opened the door.

A wary porter held out a package. 'For Señora Wilton,' he said, and disappeared like the spangles of light, and Ellie passed the parcel to her mother, who opened it at once.

Not a dainty picker of cellophane, untier of ribbon. Not mum. Rip and tear, that was her motto. Monogrammed paper flew and fluttered, ribbon dug into the package beneath and

66

there it was: an expensive sort of box, and in it a dress. She lifted it out and held it to herself.

'Oh my God,' Fiona said. 'Jean Muir.'

'Does it always work like that?' her daughter asked. 'Or do you have to rub your magic lamp first?' But her mother was sad, close to tears.

'I can't wear it,' she said. 'I can't.'

'Don't you like it?'

'I love it,' her mother said.

'Then of course you can wear it.'

But all Fiona could do was wail, 'Oh, Ellie. What am I going to do with him?'

Evening. Not really dark at all, but the fireworks boomed away even so, as he watched an elderly Daimler waddle its way to the hacienda. The chauffeur got out and opened the door, and a vision alighted – nothing so common as got out – a vision in a kaftan of gold and rose pink, and a toque like an Indian dancer's.

'Gerald, for God's sake,' Callan said. 'Not the Widow Twanky act again.'

'Embassy security thought the opposition would be looking for a little old man, so they sent a little old woman instead,' Gerald said.

'*Lady*, Gerald,' said Callan. 'You were always a lady.'

Gerald simpered. 'You are sweet,' he said. 'I delivered the fripperies.' Together they walked into the War Room.

'I had to get a chum to shop for you,' Gerald continued. 'Rather gorgeous, your little friend, but then so are the fripperies.'

He went to the great display of muskets and swords with a pistol as centrepiece, looked in the mirror next to it and removed his toque, touched up his lipstick and said, 'When I think of what I once was – but there's simply no point. We're secure, I take it? Good. If I might just recap?'

Callan waited.

'There are three – units, shall we say? As you know. Smethwick, the Englishman, Mendez, a Spaniard with disreputable friends – really quite awful, some of them—'

'And a German,' Callan said, and Gerald looked up at once.

Treat him right or live in World's End, Gerald thought. Be nice. 'Voss,' he said. 'All with one thing in common. They need money. All three. So some clever clogs – let's call him Bishop – and a person unknown, though my guess is it's Bishop's Russian counterpart – a bit shy, but weighed down with wealth – anyway, they offer Hermann the German vast sums if he'll get a team together and kill you – or kidnap you. Even better.'

'Did they say why?' Callan asked.

'Could be your treasure,' said Gerald. 'They reckon it's theirs and they want it back.'

'And then they'd kill me?' said Callan.

'Eventually.'

Callan sat motionless, impassive.

'First they'd give Oberleutnant Voss another bite at the cherry, if I may so put it.'

Callan shrugged.

'Then there's your stay in the Postdam Hilton. You'll kill Voss for that, and Bishop, and they know it – unless they kill you first.'

Callan poured out drinks and waited. There was more. Had to be.

'You realize your lady's under threat as well? Kill her and you'll go to pieces – and they know that too. You'd be a – what was it the RAF used to say? A piece of cake.'

'Not to sound nosy, Gerald old chum, but how do you know all this?'

As he spoke, a buzzer sounded, a light flashed, and a man came in.

All I bloody need, thought Callan, and aloud, 'Not now, Bernardo.'

'*Lo siento, comandante*,' said Bernardo, and bowed and left.

'Talk of angels,' Gerald said.

Callan looked at his watch. 'In my dressing room,' he said. 'I have to change.'

Mail order jeans, New England moccasins, Jermyn Street

68

shirt, crocodile belt. A few years ago, it had been C&A, but this was him, really him, thought Gerald, then Callan tied on a webbing holster that made him even more himself, and an absolute beast of a gun that somehow looked as if it enjoyed its work. A loose-fitting linen coat, and then the cheval mirror, watching himself draw, aim, draw, aim, over and over.

Gerald said, 'You *will* remember I'm on your side?'

'Do my best,' Callan said. Gerald sighed.

'Will it take long?' he asked.

'Five minutes either way,' said Callan.

Gerald looked bewildered.

'Before they're all dead – or we are. You need a minder – is that it?'

'No, no.' For once, Gerald looked furtive. 'All taken care of.'

A bit of the other? Callan wondered. When he's *working*?

'What I really need is a room to change in,' said Gerald.

'Esteban will find you somewhere.'

'Esteban?'

'Butler,' said Callan. 'Goes with the territory.'

Haciendas, thought Gerald. Lagondas. Little friends. And now butlers, bless him . . .

'Talking of staff,' he said, 'Hermann the German also has one – sounds incredible, doesn't it? A little Spanish friend who sometimes does odd jobs for him – only, sometimes Hermann forgets to pay him. Now, I never forget.'

'Ah,' said Callan.

'*Ah* just about sums it up,' said Gerald. 'So, foolish Bernardo sings *very* sweetly, if the price is right.'

'Bernardo?'

'The very same. Mendez's fee for tonight's little jaunt, for example. Rather a lot, even for you—'

'How much is a lot,' Callan asked.

'A hundred thousand dollars,' said Gerald. 'American. No cheques, no euros.'

'My best yet,' said Callan.

A long silence, then: 'Let's hope it isn't one of his better nights,' said Callan. 'He's supposed to be good.'

*　　*　　*

69

They lounged in the shade of the Lagonda: Callan, William, Mars. All three wore lightweight jackets and Mars had a golf cap as well: bright scarlet, with the letters KGB on it.

'Questions?' said Callan.

Mars yawned and stretched. 'Not really . . . There are three of them. We knock them off, shove them under the other rubbish and that's it.'

'William?'

'I drop you by the alley, check that the ladies are safe, come back and do my best.'

'That'll do me.' Callan stood up and the others followed. 'That's it then,' he said. 'Wagons roll.'

William started the car. 'I just hope we know what we're doing,' he said.

'Show some sense,' said Mars. 'If we knew what we were doing, we wouldn't be doing it.'

Fiona looked at herself in the mirror, then did a twirl. Not bad, she thought. Not bad at all – with rather a lot of help from Jean Muir. Ciggies, lighter, make-up and that was it. To carry money was ridiculous. Money was definitely Major Gotlots' department . . . Behind her, a nasty crystal vase caught the sun at last like a prism, and became a rainbow, and in the mirror she watched herself grab a vase in a flat in Bayswater – tacky room, tacky Fiona in a tacky dress – and clout darling David over the head with it. There was a gun in his hand and Guy Fawkes on the telly, and she was weeping.

Then – it was as if she'd snapped her fingers – still in that tacky room, they were dancing, the worst Astaire-Rogers ever, but they laughed – that was the point – laughed, so that the tacky room was a palace.

Another snap and she lay on the tackiest couch in the entire world, which smelled of dust and Mansion Polish and a cat yet to be deprived of its fun. At least she smelled of Nina Ricci. And he, her darling, smelled of death. There was Givenchy and Johnny Walker Black, a little, and cigarettes, but always death was the strongest, even then: arms about her, talking. Listening. Her on a grouse shoot, him helping the Russians beat Napoleon, just once. A hunt ball. Hammersmith Palais. Venice,

Iraq, New York, Bali . . . Until they ran out of places and just lay there, in a daze of happiness so intense – like an entire vintage in one glass, she thought. And then the phone rang. A very large car, the desk clerk said, and Señor Fish Moritz.

A very large man, she thought, then one more check and she was ready. They walked to the car, she and the others. No power on earth could make the Lagonda inconspicuous. It shouldered its way through the Clios and Seats, an amiable giant, but a giant even so . . .

The killing ground was just as Gerald had said it would be: an alley behind a street of shops, bars, restaurants. Rubbish skips, bin bags, junk, and all of it stinking, because that's the way death is. Dark too. Good and bad, the dark. For both sides.

The two men stood in the streetlights, fumbling for cigarettes, breathing slowly, deeply.

'Next big bang,' said Callan. 'And don't hang about.'

Fire crackers like rifle fire, and then it came. A boom from Bikini atoll, and the two men took off, racing for the shadows, and Mendez and his happy warriors were there, ready for the kill, but a great sheet of light hit the shadows, more crackers exploded, then even more. Gerald really knows how to lay on a party, thought Callan. Mendez's Marauders were too busy diving for cover to fire at the good guys.

William watched as the three of them went into the Patio Andaluz – Fiona, Ellie, Melissa, laughing, chattering, happy as foxes in a hen house – then took the Lagonda round the block. Down every alley, fireworks crackled, boomed, banged, and down Callan's alley they glowed too, but dimly, the light dying, the bangs harder, more nerve-wracking.

A body moved, then vanished, and behind it another one, slower, a gun held two-handed, sure of its target. William banged on the car horn, yelled: 'David. Behind you!' then leaped from the car. The experimental move, Callan called it – the experiment being to find out if he'd be alive thirty seconds later. The two-handed wonder dithered, then dropped. Two shots, William thought. The command from on high. Two shots, no more, no less. And fired.

Silence, maybe a whole second, then William dashed for

the alley and looked at the enemy. Two red patches, head and heart, and one of them his. David was right. He could do it – as long as he didn't think . . . Then David slammed into him like a rugby player, and an automatic ripped the silence apart, bullets smashing into the sky. They would have smashed into him.

Down the alley then, dark, but their eyes had grown used to the darkness, and they waited for Mendez and his oppo, while the fireworks blasted yet again. Pretty colours in the sky, red and yellow for Spain, green and white for Andalucia, and by their light, a shadow, a dark gleam of skin, and then three shots but no return of fire.

Fat chance, thought Mars. Three bullets in their target, all there or thereabouts, and already bleeding in a serious sort of way. He had to move if he could. Better than huddling in the gutter like a rat.

Callan took off running, blocking the last escape route Mendez had left, and Mendez cut loose again with the automatic, blasting like a maniac, and Callan sat placidly on a not-too-recent copy of *ABC*, waiting for the silence, and when it came, he called, 'Alive, you hear?' and the three men pounced, but Mendez just lay there like a drunk. Not even much pain, but he was obviously dying.

Mars opened a plastic bag, William gathered in the weapons, calling out their names: 'One Iver Johnson PP30, two Heckler and Koch 9-mill automatics, one Smith and Wesson .22 target . . .' Suddenly Mendez scuttled like a lizard towards a sawn-off shotgun, but William reached out, took away the gun. 'Now, that'll do,' he said. 'That's naughty . . . One sawn-off Remington Speedmaster . . .' and threw it to Mars.

'You want to keep them?' he asked, but Callan shook his head, and they buried guns and bodies in a rubbish skip, piling more black bags on top. As they worked, Callan said, 'Gerald reckons he's got a getaway bike.' He turned to Mendez and asked, 'Where is it? The bike?' Mendez looked away and Callan squatted beside him and spoke in Spanish. At once Mendez pointed.

'On the pavement,' said Callan.

Cautious of their clothes, William and Mars picked up Mendez. Mars said, 'You've got a bad back, I suppose.'

'Chronic,' said Callan.

They took Mendez to the bike, a BMW, spanking new, and sat him on the seat, put his hands on the handlebars. Once, he slipped, Callan grabbed him, banged him into place, and Mendez gave a sort of whistling scream – or was it a rocket?

'Callan, for God's sake!' said Mars.

'He'd have done a lot worse to Fiona – and Ellie,' Callan said, 'and anyway – where's the harm? It's only a bit of fun.' He looked at them, eyes guileless as a child's, then turned the key, pressed the starter. 'Mind how you go,' he said, and heaved Mendez into the traffic, and Mendez accelerated, not that he knew, as vans, lorries, coupés, family saloons swerved and braked as their drivers cursed.

William risked a look at Callan. There he stood, the grand-master, the best and the last, dreamily smiling, a cigarette in his mouth and a lighter in his hand that he clicked into flame. On off, on off, on off, till Mendez hit a freezer truck and the bike exploded. One more bonfire among so many.

'What time is it?' Callan asked, and still he smiled.

Easy, thought Mars. Like it's all in the day's work.

'Eight o'clock,' he said, and at once the sane Callan was back in control.

'Oh my God, she'll kill me,' he said. 'We're late.'

Seven

A vast café-dansant sort of place, thought Fiona. Dance floor, music, wine, tapas, bedlam. But a very efficient bedlam, where the wine was always there. And her chums, because Ellie was that too, and so was Melissa – and Jean Muir to make up the four. On the floor, Carmencita was dancing – white flamenco dress with scarlet dots the size of saucers, and Angel, who seemed to have strayed from a Goya painting. The music was from Bermondsey, written months ago and already old hat, but they danced a bullfight, laughing helplessly, and never once missed the beat.

Then – enter the mighty one, with attendant lords, and if the lords seemed rather shaken at first, it vanished as soon as they saw their ladies, leopards moving in on a herd of gazelles, Fiona thought, and their lord and master too. On her. It bloody better be on her. Except – no man should have the power to make her heart leap like that, not unless his did too.

Then he reached her and she smiled at him. If a diamond smiled, it would be like that, he thought. Hard, brilliant, dangerous. She got up at once to dance. Old stuff. 'My Blue Heaven.' He could handle that. No problem. *She* was the problem.

'So good of you to come,' she said. 'One feels such a fool dancing on one's own.'

'Depends on what you're dancing,' he said.

'Never mind that' – like a good sergeant flattening a clever-clogs recruit. 'Let's talk about punctuality.'

'I'm only a simple soldier, mam,' he said. 'Far too late to learn words of five syllables.'

Silently, she counted. He was right, the bastard. Even so, she laughed.

74

'That's better,' he said.

'It was either that or lie awake trying to think of an answer – and you needn't start getting ideas.'

Bloody Gerald signalling. He would be. Dressed in the full Carmen Miranda, fruit all over the place, frilled skirt, half an orange grove on his head, cherry earrings. Straight, gay, what day is it? They all come after David. Well, they couldn't have him. And no good shaking those grapefruit, Gerald darling. I've got my own, thank you very much . . .

'Oh, sod it,' said David, and at once she felt better.

'How long?' she asked. 'Five minutes?'

He nodded.

'Well, mind you mean it.'

He took her back to the table. Perfect gentlemen, the Paras – the ones who didn't use their knuckles when they walked.

'Dear boy, how *nice*,' said Gerald, and poured champagne. 'This is Pancho.'

Like a bandit from *The Magnificent Seven*, Callan thought. Sombrero, floppy moustache, bandoliers, cartridge belt, the lot.

'He's my – what's the word – my grinder.'

'Minder,' said Pancho.

'Yes, indeed,' said Gerald, and patted Pancho's cheek, then turned back to Callan. 'You're a little late. Unavoidably delayed, no doubt?'

Callan shrugged, and Gerald tried again, the first hint of worry beginning to show.

'But all is well, I trust?'

Callan looked at the fruit farm Gerald wore.

'Peachy,' he said.

'So quick,' she said. 'Three and a half minutes for a – lovers' quarrel?'

'That's up to you,' he said.

'Then you've nothing to worry about,' said Fiona. 'Not tonight.'

They danced in the old style. Gershwin, 'He Loves and She Loves', the lights dimmed, and they embraced as they danced. And then the drum roll, and the music faded as the lights grew

75

stronger, the flamenco guitars began to play and a group of young people, elegant, idle, rich – even Ellie, she thought, at least she *looks* rich – began to clap their hands to the music, flamenco style. Melissa and William, Ellie and Mars, and Angel the leader. Soon . . . soon, the hands, the guitars said, then Carmencita exploded among them like a white and scarlet bomb.

'Oh, my God,' said Fiona. 'She's wonderful. If you don't tell her you're pleased, I'll— I'll—'

'I'm pleased,' he said. 'I've never been so pleased in my entire life.'

Then the music ended and the applause began: clapping, yelling, and Callan whistled and leaped to his feet, fingers apart, until she saw him, and his hands closed and she curtseyed, blew kisses to Fiona and him, and William lifted her down from the stage. More music then. A driving beat, loud and strong. Carmencita danced again, bizarre and yet beautiful in flamenco costume, while Callan watched. Two more minutes. Beside him, Fiona and Ellie yelled at each other. It was the only way to be heard.

'Where?' Fiona screeched. 'San Lorenzo? Tell Carmencita to phone us if you need us. Where?' Her hand covered Callan's.

'At the hacienda – where else?'

Ellie kissed her mother, grinned at Callan and left with her friends.

'They're off to some madhouse on the San Lorenzo road,' said Fiona. 'Carmencita promises she won't dance.'

'Then she won't,' Callan said.

But still she fretted. 'All the same – it's pretty rough, Ellie said.'

'No doubt,' said Callan. 'Three of the four loveliest women in the place. Don't tell me. But look who they're with. John, William, Angel. Anyone who takes on those three *has* to be barmy.'

She relaxed. 'True, oh mighty one,' she said.

He looked bewildered. She liked it when he looked bewildered.

'Mighty?' he said.

'You got medals for it. Want to try for another?'

'Try, sure,' he said. 'I'm not so young as I was.' He rose to his feet.

'Not here,' she said. 'Mustn't frighten the horses.'

'Absolutely not,' he said. 'Shocking thing to do.'

She rose and smiled. Perhaps the unkindest smile he'd ever seen, and then it came to him. She's thinking about George.

'This punch-up you're after,' he asked. 'Does it have rules?'

'No.'

'I know just the place,' he said.

The Lagonda turned into the driveway, and a man in battle fatigues seemed to grow out of the ground. Both he and the machine pistol he carried seemed to know their business.

'Callan,' said The Mighty One, '*y mi señora.*'

The guard came closer and checked them. '*Buenos noches, Señora,*' he said. '*Señor Comandante.*'

Fiona eased herself into the cushions. Really, she thought, it's like sitting on moonbeams, and bang on cue, the moonbeams appeared.

'"Callan," you said. "And his lady."'

'Do you mind?'

The car rounded a bend and she could see the junk pile again, far away, like some lunatic's rocket he'd made himself. The mighty one didn't even look. George would have been beside himself. George could do that . . .

Then, Come on, old girl. You're with the one and only . . . Who needs George?

'Of course I don't mind,' she said. 'I love it, being your lady. What now?'

He eased the car to a stop. No sign of the junk heap, and just as well. Definitely out of place. Phallic. There was no changing that, but all that junk. Like a randy tramp. And then: *Stop it.* You're scared. All right. But it's far too late for that. And anyway, he can't eat you . . . But how marvellous if he could.

'We wait,' he said, and looked at his watch. 'Not long.'

A sunbed the size of a squash court, and they lay on it and waited. For what? A chorus line? Strippers? A randy tramp?

He drew her to him on the bed. Around them were a million roses, and his arms were gentle and the show began. One by one, birds sang: drab little birds with the voices of angels. 'But surely they're nightingales?' she said, and he nodded. 'We could be in Sussex . . . Thank God we're not.'

He was touching her and it was utter bliss. Not like some, because he knew how to touch.

Oh my God, my dress, she thought, and found she wasn't wearing one. Ah well. I'm sorry, Ms Muir, but just for once I have to do what I'm told. He's got medals and things.

Then the nightingales changed key and her bra came off and a shower of rose petals touched her – and how the *hell* had he fixed that? Even for a major in the Paras . . . Follow that. And he did. She yelled very softly and said, 'Wait . . . You said you'd wait.'

'Tomorrow,' he said. 'We'll wait tomorrow.'

No groping, no fumbling, just bliss from the very first second. Guaranteed, one-hundred-proof bliss. Accept no substitute. On and on, till a cloud covered the moon and the nightingales rolled up their music.

'Great galloping gollywogs,' she said.

'Now what? Not the dress?'

'The dress is later. Us. You and me.'

'What about you and me?'

'It's wonderful,' she said.

'Well, of course it is.'

Bewildered, poor darling. Medals and all. How to explain? 'I didn't know, you see. I didn't bloody know.'

'Oh, come *on*,' said Callan.

'I didn't,' she said. 'All I knew was George performing the "Anvil Chorus".'

'The what?' More bewildered than ever.

'*Il Trovatore*,' said Fiona, and sang the tune.

'Woosh bang, woosh bang, woosh bang bang – and then the big finish – Well, the finish anyway . . . What is it the Yanks say?'

Gently, seriously, he said, '*Wham bam thank you, ma'am.*'

'That's the one,' she said. 'Except, with George, it was,

Goodnight, old girl. And once, I swear to God, it was, *Well, that's that. Time for sleepy byes.*'

Callan said, 'He must have been mad.'

'No,' she said. 'I was mad. He was queer.' She twisted in his arms to face him. 'You wouldn't do that to me, would you?'

'I couldn't,' Callan said. He kissed her gently. A friend's kiss.

'Do you know, I believe that? I really do,' she said, at once happy and surprised. And then, 'I left it a bit late, but not too late, thank God. Like number nine buses.'

'*Buses?*' said Callan.

Bewildered, bless him, and that made it twice in one night. Not bad . . . Thirty–love, major, darling.

'Not a sign of one, and then they all come together. What now?'

'You don't like it here?'

'I love it here,' she said, 'but I have the feeling there's more.'

'Could be,' he said. 'Fancy a swim?'

'*A swim?*'

'You do it in water.'

'I know what you do it in,' she said. 'Have you had a good look at me?'

'I've looked at nothing else all evening,' he said.

'Yes . . . Well . . . Never mind that . . . Well, not for now, anyway. Darling, I can't possibly go skinny-dipping. I'm forty. I've had two children. Stretch marks that would impress a giraffe.'

'What's that got to do with it?' he asked, and she hugged him.

'What's that got— Oh, what bliss you are,' she said, and then, 'Do they know about bliss where you come from?'

'Where I come from, they wouldn't know about bliss if you served it with chips,' he said. 'Let's have that swim.'

And he picked her up, just like the last time, no straining, no grunts and groans, just floating like a leaf in the breeze, and her arm came round his neck, like a parcel from Harvey Nick's, and they reached the pool and he threw her in and even that was a kind of flying.

'My God, it's *warm*,' she said, and he dived in beside her, and they swam side by side, then he hauled himself out and watched her till she swam to where he waited and again he lifted her, wrapped her in a vast towel like another parcel, from Bond Street, say. (Yes, yes, Ms Muir, your turn next.)

'It won't last, you know,' she said.

'What won't?'

She sat on some sort of a box contraption, and still he looked at her. As if I was put together by Watteau on a day when it all came right, she thought.

'You,' she said. 'Me. I'll go on loving you, of *course*. I mean, what chance have I got? But I won't go on being nice. I can't. God didn't put me here to be nice.'

'The devil did that,' said Callan.

'My God!' she said. 'You understand. But it won't make a scrap of difference.'

She pulled the towel closer round her, like a sari. 'I'm cold,' she said.

'No wonder,' said Callan. 'You're sitting on an icebox.'

She jumped to her feet. 'Swine,' she said. 'You could have told me.'

'You didn't ask,' he said, and then, 'Your rules.' They were too.

'Look in the box,' he said.

Champers, of course, which should have been a cliché, but this wasn't a man for clichés. The label a glowing gold, and the letters the blue of the sky at that very moment. FD intertwined, and below, 1996.

He took the bottle and stinging cold glasses, and poured.

'I suppose the '96 was a marvellous year?' she said, and he nodded. 'And you own all that's left?'

'We both do,' he said. 'And don't start. It's a drink. Now, either you and me are what they call an item, or you're stringing me along something rotten. Well?'

'All right, we're an item,' she said, 'but I—'

'Then drink your nice cava.'

It was a walloper. Smooth, though. Easy. Like him when he— 'Cava?' she said. 'This is Spanish?'

'Cataluña's best,' he said.

'My God, it has to be,' she said. 'So, how many have you
– *we* – got?' He shrugged. 'A dozen?'
'Hard to say,' he said. 'We own the vineyard.'
And that, she thought, is the meaning of the word *rich*.
'Let's talk about dresses,' she said, and he waited. Best to
get it over with.
'A bit personal, wasn't it?'
'You had a problem,' he said. 'So I put Gerald on to it.'
'*Gerald?*'
'Queens love choosing dresses,' he said. 'If he got it
wrong . . .' He shrugged. 'But he got it dead right, and you
know it.'
She brooded, then smiled.
'MGM, would it be?' she said. 'Two girls and one dress.
Lauren Bacall and a promising newcomer called Monroe. And
two chaps – their chaps. David Niven. Jack Lemmon. And
when one of the girls has a date, it's her turn for the dress
– until the night they both have a date. At the same party.'
'Wilton Productions present *The Dress*,' he said. 'Starring
Fiona Wilton. Directed by Fiona Wilton. Script by Fiona
Wilton. With Ellie Wilton, featuring John Mars, William
Fitzmaurice, Roger Bullevant.'
'You honestly think he would?'
'Roger? He'd love it . . . And then at the end, Fight
Arrangers – D. Major and F. Rugg. It can't miss. Maybe I
will buy MGM.'
'But you can't,' she said. 'You *mustn't*. I mean. You *are*
joking?'
He shrugged. 'And, just in case you're not – I know it's not
possible, but just in case – I won't have it. Now, I mean that.'
'When you were little,' he said. 'Did you have a nanny?'
'What's that got to do with it?'
'I thought you did,' he said, and she threw her glass at him
and he grabbed her, held her still.
'The pool,' he whispered. 'Watch.'
An eagle owl. Huge. Majestic. One cut of its wings and it
planed over the rose garden, then hooted its disgust. Not even
a biscuit. The wings flicked once more, angry, disdainful, and
it glided into the shadows.

'My God, how marvellous,' she said. 'Do you own him too?'

'Nobody owns him,' said Callan. 'He may own me some-times, when he's hungry, but that's it.' And then. 'Good luck to him. Why don't we go back to my place and try out a few love scenes for your movie?'

'You're on,' she said, 'if you can carry me that far.'

And up she went past that bloody bonfire again, and into the hacienda to a door half ajar, and a room that was elegant blue and yellow. A ceiling fan as soft as a lullaby.

'This isn't yours,' she said.

'Guest room. Mine's a little more austere.'

'So am I,' she said. 'I'll sleep in your bed. F&D, remember?'

Carried across the threshold. What a man. Even so, austere was right. Austere walls, ceiling, furniture. Even the floor. And two pictures. Rembrandt's *Night Watch* and a bunch of cavalrymen on grey horses who look even madder than me, she thought. Right up there in David's class. He put her down at last. '*The Charge of the Scots Greys at Waterloo*,' he said. 'Lady Butler.'

'They look as if they're watching a football match on horseback.'

'It's a present from Roger,' he said. 'She was pretty good at uniforms.'

'And the Rembrandt. More soldiers.'

'Half my life,' he said. 'The rest was the nick.'

'Then why—'

'I mean, just look at them,' said Callan. 'A more untidy shower of no-hope deadbeats I never want to see. I drill them sometimes. Line them up in parade order, kit inspection, the works. Haircut that man. Those boots are filthy. Look at those buttons, Sergeant Major. Hasn't he heard of Mepo? You may have broken your mother's heart, but you won't break mine, so watch it. Now then.'

He smiled.

'Sort of a lullaby,' she said and lay on the bed, and he joined her. Gentle again. No rush.

'The game,' he said.

'Dr Rabin's? What about it?'

'I can't do it!'

'You're a marvellous supporting cast.'

He shrugged. 'That's all right then. But with me it's got to be real.'

'You think I don't know?'

'Don't I ever scare you?' he asked.

She thought about it. Another reason to love her: no easy lie. She *thought*.

'No more than I scare you,' she said. 'You could kill me with one hand, maybe even one finger . . . but you wouldn't. Oh, come here.'

She cuddled him as if he was an eight-year-old Ellie whose hamster had died, until he said, 'One last question. Do you mind?'

'What happened to Ellie's brother?'

'How in the world—' he said.

'Because you're such a clever bastard. You never miss a trick. A boy. Stillborn. Ellie was three . . . and George went off the whole idea. Not even one chorus on the anvil. It has its good points, being a chap . . . That's all I want to say about it.'

'God knows, it's enough, poor love,' he said, and kissed her.

'Save your strength,' she said. 'You see, it's like this. After I kissed the frog—'

'That's me, I suppose.'

'It better be,' she said, '—and you turned into a handsome prince, I sort of knew there'd be lots of you-know-whatting. And I was right, bless you. And when we did sleep, I still wanted us to be together – starkers as Indian statues.'

'Didn't they wear funny hats?'

'I'll have to think about that,' she said.

Eight

She awoke to a rhythmic metallic thump, and thought of machines that knocked holes in roads, powered ships, bent girders. She found her bathrobe and went out into the hallway, looked into the gym, where the mighty one was doing things with weights that looked really quite awful. He finished at last and turned on a shower that hit like a fire hose. He's not human, she thought. He can't be. But, oh my God, he's gorgeous, bless him. She waited till he'd put on his bathrobe then, 'He left me!' she cried. 'Abandoned me. Our first night and he casts me off like an old shoe!'

Still dripping wet, he picked her up and carried her to the weights machines.

'Not even a thank you,' she called, booming like a theatrical dame. 'Not even goodbye.'

He put the weights into her hands.

'Lift them,' he said. 'Never mind the Shakespeare. Lift!'

Well, I tried, she thought, but I couldn't budge the bloody things. 'I can't.'

'Then listen,' he said, and when she started to speak, 'I said, listen.'

His hands covered hers, but gently, and the weights moved.

'Every day I do this,' he said, 'and every day I shoot with a Smith and Wesson magnum. Thirty years old and as good as new and I wish I could say the same. But I'm the richest man we know – except for Roger – and you're here and I'm beginning to believe it. Leave you? Even I'm not that stupid.'

'You're not stupid at all,' she said, 'and I love what you're saying. But you hadn't finished, had you?'

He waited.

'Voss,' she said. 'He's going to try to kill you.'

'That was last week. Now he's going to try for you and Ellie as well.'

'When I was poor,' she said. '—Yesterday was it? Nobody wanted to kill me. Even the bank let me live till I'd paid off the overdraft.' She looked at him. 'So troubled, poor love. Don't worry,' she said. 'It won't happen. We couldn't possibly be killed by Voss. Too lowering . . .'

She kissed him and her hands grasped his robe, then opened it a little and looked at a neat row of burn marks, reached out to touch, then: 'Oh, I'm sorry,' she said. 'Do you mind?'

'Of course I don't mind,' he said. 'This is us. You and me.'

She touched them.

'They're like little bits of marble,' she said. 'Couldn't the surgeons do *anything*?'

'They fixed everything else,' said Callan. 'They were the best. The nicest too. But those bits beat even them. Oh boy . . . What a makeover that was.'

She took fire at once. A lighted match in a petrol can.

'Stop that!' she yelled. 'Stop it! You hear me? You won.' Then the fire died. She kissed the marks Voss had made so precisely. 'I'm sorry,' she said.

His arms came round her.

'You didn't know,' he said. 'How could you?' Then he smiled. 'Let's have breakfast,' he said. 'Emilio makes his own croissants.'

On the hillside, as close to the bonfire as he dared, Voss thought it through. Bishop never stopped telling him. 'Think it through,' but Bishop was in St Petersburg, eating caviar. And Bishop didn't know about his failures. Not yet. Better think about a success. Not the Wilton cow. It would take a squadron of tanks to get to her: CIA, SAS, wrapped round her like a wall. *And* her daughter. His ex. More bad news. Nothing now to stop her telling all to the papers. She could buy the bloody papers, so rich he was. Callan. Screaming when the Zippo burned, and now it was all laughter. He, Voss, would be the one who screamed. Kill Callan.

It was the only way to be safe. Callan dead and Bishop happy.

He took out the glasses and looked into the hacienda's garden. Bernardo on his knees, grubbing up weeds. Weeds and kneeling. That was Bernardo. Pretty though, even now. As he watched, Bernardo stood up and stretched, walked out of the garden. Time to go. London, and hash to sell, and jollies. Wasn't that the word?

Then he stumbled and fell like a clown, into a thorn bush that was no more than dry, dead wood which crackled as he struggled to be free, dry soil falling on the bonfire. Two guardia, a thin one having a nap, and a fat one tugging at the pistol in his holster.

Above them, Mars watched, then yawned. It had been a long, long time since he'd yawned lying down . . . *Christ that my love were in my arms. And I in my bed again*, as we cultured chappies say. Fat chance. But at least it was funny. Old Vossers leaping from crag to crag, and the fat guardia looking at his pistol, trying to find the trigger. Time to go.

Mars took off over the brow of the hill, then up and over and out of sight. Somewhere a gun banged. Just like the pictures, he thought. Keystone Cops . . . On to where the Morgan waited, faithful steed, and a path more rock than earth. Not that the Morgan minded bumps. It could bump back and mean it. Every time. Then the road improved, and just ahead a chopper sailed out of nowhere, like they do, and gleamed in the early sunlight. Nearer to heaven, and why not? The pilot's name was Angel.

'Another croissant?' said Callan.

'I shouldn't,' she said. 'I really shouldn't.'

He passed them to her, and the butter, and Emilio's very own cherry jam. Fiona scowled at him, and spread butter like plaster on a brick.

'It's disgusting,' she said. 'If you think I—'

The mobile rang and Callan laid it on the table.

'Wendy to Peter,' said the voice. 'Report from Lost Boy One.'

Wearily Callan said, 'Just tell it, Gerald. I'm still asleep.'

'Hook's crocodile negative presence,' said the voice. 'Ditto alarm clock. Dest Londinium.'

'What the hell's that?' said Callan.

'Destination London,' said Fiona, fascinated.

'Chance of Episcopus,' said the voice. 'And remember Scouts' motto. Teachers' too.'

'Gerald, will you for God's sake speak English,' said Callan, and the line went dead as Callan turned to Fiona.

'Episcopus?' he said. 'Would that be Bishop?'

She nodded.

'That's all I bloody need,' said Callan. 'I was going to take you to bed and listen to the nightingales.'

'Nightingales? At this hour?'

'We could wait,' said Callan. The phone rang. 'Gerald, I'm warning you,' he said, then, 'Oh, sorry, John. It's just I've had Gerald on my back being . . .' He looked at Fiona.

'Whimsical,' she said.

'Being whimsical. It's too bloody early to be whimsical. Let's have it.'

The telephone yacked and slowly he relaxed.

'You saw him in? Of course you did. Excuse the question . . . See him on to the plane then go to HQ. Have some breakfast. You did a nice job.'

He hung up.

'Coming on a treat,' he said.

'John?'

'Mm. Tailed Herr Voss. Him and Angel. All the way to the airport. Voss picked up a passenger. Bernardo – suitcase, flight bag, the lot – so, we're one slave short.'

'But why? Leg it, I mean.'

'My guess is violence,' said Callan. 'I wouldn't want Bernardo in the way if I was in a fight. His job's being cute.'

'Let me tell you something nice,' she said. 'Last night—'

'*Nice*?' said Callan. 'It was wonderful!'

'Marvellous,' she said. 'Not an anvil in sight. Please *listen*.'

'Yes, miss,' said Callan.

'My father was an earl,' said Fiona.

'He never—'

She talked on, her words smashing his. The only way. 'So last night you didn't just you-know-what with a Sloane. You're climbing the ladder, Major. You did it with a Lady, capital L. Me. Lady Fiona Wilton.'

'It's a lovely thing to know,' he said, 'but it doesn't make it better. Nothing could. Not a thing.'

She smiled. *Olé*, comandante.

'All the same – talk about the princess and the peasant,' he said.

'Except this time the peasant's got all the dosh.'

Then Esteban appeared, took one look, bowed and kept on walking. A treasure.

'There's another thing,' Fiona said. 'Esteban. What do I call him? The butler?'

'He's sort of the sergeant major,' said Callan. '*Jefe de los criados*. Just call him Esteban. What about him?'

'And there's Emilio too,' said Fiona. 'Are you sure they won't mind?'

'Mind?' said Callan. 'They've been dropping hints ever since they saw you. The way they see it – money's one thing, but class is another. You can't buy class.'

'You can try,' she said.

His turn to smile, but then the phone rang and he reached for it and sighed.

'Casa Fiona,' he said, and she blinked. 'Yes, she's here. Everything's OK . . . And you? Great . . . I'll put her on.'

He handed over the phone and spoke to her. Gently. Easily.

'Ellie,' he said. 'Now, don't start. She's fine. They're all fine.'

Fiona didn't believe a word.

'Ellie?' she said. 'What's happening? Oh, breakfast. So are we, but we can always— If you're sure. Fine . . . About an hour. Bye, darling.' She gave back the mobile. 'How odd.'

Callan waited.

'There's a message for me at the hotel.'

'Want me to drive you over, or would you sooner go yourself?'

'You, please.'

'I thought you liked driving,' he said.

'What *I* like driving is something just a little more demure. Not that upper-class raging maniac. One look at that Lagonda and I just know it went to Eton.'

She yawned and stretched. 'You drive,' she said. 'You've faced more raging maniacs than I've had hot dinners.'

Callan took one look and went back inside for his camera. This, after all, was history happening before his eyes. Beside the Lagonda, Gerald's ageing Daimler was parked, and beside the Daimler, Gerald, in tracksuit and trainers, was doing the wariest warm-up exercises he'd ever seen.

'Are you sure you're alright?' he asked.

'Well, of course I'm not alright,' said Gerald. 'That's why I take exercise. Not the actual running about – I've got Pancho for that – too exhausting . . .' He looked at his watch. 'Late, stupid fellow. He's dreadfully out of condition. No . . . It's the clothes I like. So *butch*.'

Glass flashed like a heliograph, and Callan covered his eyes.

'Gerald, for God's sake,' he said.

'Pancho. I'm trying to work out where Voss takes cover before he starts his flashing.'

'Voss flew to London.'

'He booked a return ticket by phone.'

'Just one?'

'And a single.'

'Oh dear, oh dear,' said Callan.

'Can we talk?' Gerald asked.

'Fiona said ten minutes,' said Callan, 'but that was ages ago. Better make it quick.'

'Smethwick,' Gerald said. 'We're keeping an eye on him. Sent him a couple of clients. They're buying a property. A Miss Hunter and a Miss Klein.'

'Naomi? Lives with Roger. I had her down as Mossad. One of Avram's Merry Persons.'

'I rather think she is . . . But he owes us a favour. You're thinking of all that filthy lucre of yours?'

Callan nodded.

'Mossad doesn't steal,' said Gerald.

'Avram might. He's skint.'

Gerald looked at him. 'I'll check again. You know, for an agent, you have the most extraordinary antennae—'

'I'm not an agent,' said Callan. 'I'm a thief.'

Gerald winced.

The trouble was, she had nothing to wear, the Jean Muir was at the cleaner's, and she couldn't start the *I need a dress* nonsense again. Not in two million quid's worth of real estate.

Improvise, she thought. That's the ticket. Rosebuds in her bra and a linen curtain for a sarong. Not bad, she thought. The curtain was hot, but she could take it off in the car . . .

Gerald was still doing his cautious warm-ups. A good act, Callan thought, but it did go on a bit.

'Smethwick doesn't like you,' Gerald said. 'Doesn't like you at all.'

'I don't even know him,' Callan said.

'He knows you . . . He and that ghastly Smacker. You stole their old-age pension.'

'*The Bimbo Book of Royals.*'

'The very same. You're nowhere near his Christmas-card list.'

A light beam flickered across his face, and he brushed it away as if it was a wasp.

'Pancho's a pest,' he said. 'A ten-year-old pest. He'll be yelling for a catapult next.'

'Yo-yo,' said Callan. 'He's not ready for a catapult.'

Gerald looked up. 'You mean it?' Callan nodded, and Gerald sighed . . .

Mars bought a *Daily Mail*, a paperback, a cup of coffee, as Voss waited in the ticket queue, and Bernardo counted the minutes before it was time to scream. Shot in the arm time. Voss looked at Bernardo as often as he dared. He had a problem and he knew it, thought Mars.

*   *   *

90

Pancho clocked in at last. Tracksuit, trainers, and still that ridiculous moustache, as if he'd glued a dead mouse to his upper lip.

'And about time,' said Gerald. 'How am I today?'

Pancho did everything but laugh out loud. This time he had all the cards.

'Still a bit on the flabby side, sir.'

'Bitch,' said Gerald, but Pancho was staring past him at Fiona, all flowers and curtains, and a Panama hat with an MCC ribbon that Gerald had coveted for months. She had never looked more gorgeous, thought Callan. But of course she had. Last night in a Jean Muir creation, a towel, nothing at all. She always looked gorgeous. Callan began to think of sapphires set in yellow gold, then Pancho gave a sort of groan. Jaw dropped halfway to his stomach, eyes sticking out like chapel hat pegs.

'On your bike,' Callan said, and at once Auntie Gerald took Pancho by the hand.

'Yes, come along,' he said, 'and I'll buy you a yo-yo . . .'

'Driving away my public?' she said.

'Gerald's buying him a yo-yo instead,' said Callan.

She giggled. 'So, you like the outfit?'

'It's terribly you,' he said. 'Give us a twirl.'

Two safety pins and a bit of scotch tape, she thought. But he's earned his treat. She twirled, and he thought *lots* of sapphires.

'The flasher was at it again,' she said.

'That was Pancho. Gerald was working out where Voss takes cover.'

'Looking for clues?'

'It works sometimes – only Voss cleared up when he'd finished. Every time. What he couldn't burn he carried.'

'Burn?' Fiona said. 'Here?'

'He likes burning things.' Callan said.

He bent and picked up a handful of dry leaves, tinder dry, then: 'You really want to see this?'

They did it to him, she thought, whatever it is. That bastard Voss. Even so, she had to see, to listen. If he wants to talk, try to hear him out, Rabin had said. Don't nag. Just listen. Take whatever scraps you can get . . .

Callan crushed the leaves in his palm, put them on a whatsit – sundial – on a stone shaft, produced the magnifying glass, and it happened in minutes. The bits of leaf smouldered and he added more leaves, waited for the flame, added a tiny twig that glowed red almost at once. 'Simple,' he said.

'Oh my God!' she said and held him close, so close. He was vulnerable at last. Her body smelled of suntan oil and Nina Ricci and sunlight, and she kissed him.

'You sure you want to go to the hotel?' he asked.

'Oh you,' she said. 'But please, can we look at the horses first?'

'Sure,' he said. 'Want to tell me why?'

'They're innocent,' she said.

The paperback's title was *Celibacy. Is It The Answer?* Why ask me, thought Mars. I don't even know the question. Except that Ellie would be in there somewhere, and no way was celibacy the answer to Ellie.

He looked up. Voss too was drinking coffee, and smoking a cigarette by a No Smoking sign. Then an airport policeman went to him and asked for a light. Spain was still like that sometimes. Marvellous. But, oh my God, where was Bernardo? Not a sign. Dismissed, his service career in ruins. And then Bernardo reappeared – but what a change. Hands steady, shoulders back, and a smile a double-glazing salesman would have been proud of. *Servicios*, thought Mars. A cubicle just for one, and a blissful, blissful injection with a brand new needle, then chocks away and Cloud Nine taxis to the runway.

In the real world there were aircraft too, and Voss hustled him into the departure lounge. Breakfast, thought Mars, and binned the paperback – Ellie was a great reader – then swerved to avoid a mechanized trolley like a dodgem car. On it, in solitary splendour, a dwarf sat, dressed to kill. Versace suit, silk shirt, old Etonian bow tie. A king on his way to be crowned. The entire airport lounge gawked like yokels. Including me, thought Mars. But I'm hungry.

The palominos were as mouth-watering as ever, and this time

she felt that she could ask. After all, I live here, she thought, and those darlings need work.

'Ride?' he said. 'Well, sure. Pick where you like.'

'I've got the kit at home,' she said.

'You are at home,' he said. 'All the same – send for your stuff and use boots and jeans while you're waiting. There's a geezer in Seville does boots, they tell me. I'll lend you the dosh. You can hardly ask Esteban.'

'Lend?' she said. 'You mean pay back?'

'Well, of course pay back,' said Callan. 'I only wish I could give them to you, but it's been a terrible year. Gazpacho on the marimbas, and what it did to the maracas—'

She swung at him but he caught her wrist.

'Wait till you get your gloves,' he said. 'How many times . . . And anyway, you wouldn't last two rounds in that rig.'

'You still like it then?'

'No,' said Callan. 'I don't like it at all. I love it.'

When they got to the hotel lounge, she turned every head in the place, and walked slowly, elegantly, the way Sloanes walked in her day, because Daddy signed the cheque, but raced down the bedroom corridor as if the Martians had landed.

Straight into an empty room, neatly made, coverlet in place – an alibi in itself – and her daughter taking breakfast with baa-lamb John on the balcony. Shirts and shorts, and for Ellie, a scratch pad and pencil, expounding over a map of what appeared to be Australia, and even at that moment her mother thought, Ellie, for God's *sake*. Not *now*.

'Why, Mum,' Ellie said. 'How naughty you look. Little Miss Muffet on speed.'

'Never mind that,' said Fiona. 'Just tell me. You know how I hate these messages from nowhere.'

Mars rose to his feet. This was no place for a peace-loving lad. 'Time I was off,' he said.

'*Utrunque Parata*,' said Callan. Ready for anything, in Para speak.

'*Non illegitimi sed carborundum*,' Mars said, and left to find some peace, as Fiona began to remove her bra. Nothing sexy, thought Callan. More a declaration of war.

'*Mum* . . .' Ellie's voice was imploring.

'Are we playing the game?' asked Callan. 'Are we being silly buggers again?'

The look he got was a blast from a fury, then slowly it softened, just a little.

'You're up to something,' she said. 'Something I won't like, and if I'm right, so help me God, I'll finish up starkers.'

'Maybe Ellie could join you. Me too, if you like.'

Fiona left them. When it came to exits, she was premier league.

Ellie said, 'You've done it this time,' and almost at once there was a yell from the bedroom. It sounded like *Aaagh!* he thought, then she yelled, 'They're all locked. I can't budge the bloody things.' She appeared at the door. 'Come and open them, you bastard.'

'Bastard yourself,' said Callan. 'I was an orphan.'

Still yelling, she said, 'Sorry. I didn't mean *that. Sorry.* Now, open those locks before I send for a sledgehammer.'

The bedroom was stacked full with a Vuitton trunk and cases.

'What a snob you are,' said Fiona. 'Nothing but Vuitton as far as the eye can see.' He began to unlock it all, and despite herself she said, 'I didn't know Vuitton made a trunk like that.'

'They don't,' said Callan.

She yelled again, but what was meant to be rage sounded more like despair.

'They're going back,' she said.

'You want me to lock it all up again?'

'We'll look first,' she said. 'No harm in looking.' And then to Ellie. 'Over here, you. I don't trust you. I love you, but I don't trust you. What a world. So sad.' She turned to the trunk. 'My God, it's vast. What on earth can we do with it?'

'We can always live in it after they throw us out of here,' said Ellie.

Fiona lifted the lid. The trunk was filled with coats, dresses, trousers, skirts. They knelt by the gleaming leather and Ellie read out the names like a litany: 'Jean Muir, Gucci, Armani, Nicole Farhi, Versace, Dior, Chanel.' Silent, bewildered, Fiona looked at Callan as her daughter opened the next case. Shoes: 'Gucci, Lacoste, Bruno Magli.' And then underwear: 'Janet Reger, La Perla . . .'

Her mother turned to Callan. 'How could you?' she said. 'You know I can't take. Only give. And, if that's crazy, that's what I am.'

'You're not the only one,' said Callan.

'Yes. Alright. But you can take, too.'

'I can do a bit more than that,' said Callan.

He looked strong, fit and so sane. Whatever it was, it was coming now. She turned to her daughter.

'Ellie, darling,' she said.

'No,' Callan said. 'Ellie stays.'

So it was war. 'Let's try on some clothes,' she said, pulled dresses from the trunk, began once more to remove her bra.

'Mum, *please*,' said Ellie.

'It isn't that hot,' said Callan. 'Knock it off.' But she turned away.

'Look,' he said, 'if you're going in for lap dancing, you need a lap.' He turned to Ellie. 'Know any fat guys? I mean, your mum's just a beginner and—'

Fiona put her hands to her face. Straw hat, roses, curtains and all, she was still beautiful, he thought, as Ellie embraced her. Her turn to be Mum.

'It's all right,' she said. 'Honestly. It's just that – not even you can hurt Dad now – so why bother trying?'

Fiona looked up at Callan. No tears. Only pain . . .

'She knows, doesn't she? Our first date and the game and the laughing academy . . .'

'Ellie knows the lot,' he said. 'How could I lie to her?'

Gently she moved away from Ellie.

'If it wasn't for that bastard,' she said, and nodded at Callan, 'I'd still be shattered. Bits of me all over the floor.' She turned to Callan. 'But you're still a bastard. I want a drink.'

Callan went to the telephone and she threw a wall plaque at him and Ellie yelled, 'David. Look out.'

At once, Callan swirled like a fish in a tank, and for a second looked at Fiona as he would at Voss, then other missiles flew, ashtrays, a guidebook, an empty vase. When she could find no more, he said, 'Gin and tonic all right?' When he had gone, Ellie said, 'I love you, Mum – really and truly – and I don't want to worry you, but I'm starting to love your boyfriend as well.'

'Dear God, how lucky I am,' her mother said, and found another vase, crystal and very nasty, and went to the door.

'Then why—' Ellie said.

'Always play hard to get when you can,' said her mother.

Callan was headed to where Mars sat at the bar. She let fly with the vase, and Callan ducked, just in time. The vase hit a fuse box and burst like a frag bomb. At once, the lights went out, the fans stopped spinning. Again Callan looked at his ladies.

'Any preference?' he asked.

'One Bombay gin, one Larios,' Fiona called, as Mars came up to him.

'Get that, will you?' he said. 'And a large Johnny Walker Black.'

'Why is Fiona dressed like that?' Mars asked.

'She says it's hot.'

'Well, so it is,' said Mars. 'She's just buggered up the air conditioning.'

Around them the jolly hols brigade stirred fretfully. It looked all right, looked great, in fact, but they couldn't hear. Then the woman in the fantastic beach outfit whistled and Callan looked up and said irritably, 'What now?' and they relaxed. They could hear perfectly.

'Make them large ones,' the woman said. 'And no more knickers in fancy cases.'

'Is that just you – or Ellie and me as well?'

'I don't give a monkey's manoeuvre,' Fiona said. 'Just do it.'

The crowd murmured its appreciation. Some of the women applauded.

Callan sighed. 'You heard the lady. And do something about these people. Tell them who we are.'

'Who are we?' Mars asked.

'How the hell do I know? In my report, I've said you're resourceful. Now's your chance to prove it.'

In Ellie's room, Fiona sprawled on a chair, talking because her daughter listened, but Ellie butted in at last. Had to.

'Mum, I know all this,' she said. 'And anyway, it's Dr Rabin you should be telling it to.'

'That man terrifies me,' Fiona said.

'*Dr Rabin*?'

'The mad major.'

'David would never hurt you,' Ellie said. 'He couldn't.'

'He'd hurt himself instead,' said Fiona. 'That's what terrifies me.'

Then Callan walked in. Wary, Ellie thought. The Para look, and just as well.

'You took your time,' said her mother.

'The barmen were all busy playing with the ice machine.'

'What's wrong with it?' Ellie asked.

'Your mum buggered it up,' said Callan, and turned to Fiona. 'All right. You don't like the dresses, we'll change them. Only, stop buggering up the ice machine.'

'The dresses are marvellous,' she said. 'It's just—'

But then Mars came in with the drinks and Callan beamed at him. 'Your idea's a cracker,' he said. 'Find William and Melissa. Mess jackets for you two and a frilly apron for Melissa, and not much else. Wine. Red and white plonk, and that fizz we don't like. Not the good stuff. Too many punters.'

'And the movie?' Mars asked.

'All-star cast, but your lips are sealed. Tell them it'll cost millions. Punters love those words.' He looked at his watch. 'We'll move off in an hour.'

Mars looked at *his* watch. 'Sir,' he said. 'Thirteen twenty hours.'

'On the dot,' said Callan.

'Sir,' said Mars, and stiffened to attention, then left.

'So, we're back in the army,' Fiona said.

'Some of us never left,' said Callan, and fetched the smallest case from the bedroom.

97

'Bloody fool,' he said.

'*John*?' She sounded appalled.

'You,' said Callan. 'If you'd kept your boobs under control, that vase would have got me.' He turned to Ellie. 'Get your mum's robe, would you, love?'

Ellie scurried out. She didn't want to miss a word.

'We may as well finish it now,' said Callan. 'What do you call this thing?'

'A bandbox,' Fiona said. 'But don't ask me why.'

He gave it to her, and she opened it. It was filled with perfume and make-up in jars, tubes, boxes.

'Open it,' he said. 'The one on the left. The night cream. Pull it towards you. *Gently*, you cack-handed idiot.'

A tray came out of the bandbox's base, and on it a leather case, flanked by smaller cases.

'You swine!' she said. 'Cartier.'

'Open it,' said Callan, and she did so, as Ellie came in with the robe.

'Was this the one?' she said, then, 'Oh my God!'

They both looked at a Cartier necklace, bracelet, earrings.

'I should throw it away,' Fiona said.

'Suit yourself,' said Callan. 'The firm can afford it. It's yours to wear.'

'You rotten pig,' she said. 'It isn't it isn't it isn't.'

'It will be when I sign the cheque,' he said.

'So, now you think you're buying me.'

Callan sighed, then it was his turn to yell. The yell of the sergeant he once had been. 'Will you for Gawd's sake belt up,' he roared, and then, more gently, 'Please?' and Fiona nodded. 'Five minutes?' Another nod. 'Let's try.' He sipped at his Scotch. 'This business, Roger's and mine – it's big,' he said.

'Vast,' Fiona said, then, 'Oh, sod it!' and clapped a hand to her mouth.

'I'll give you that one,' Callan said. 'It *is* vast. And I want you in it. Two reasons. One – because I do. Wherever I am, whatever I'm doing, I want you there. Part of it. Part of *me*. That's far and away the most important reason – though, mind you, the other one's important too. You'll be just right for the business . . . Not what you'd take out – what you'd put in.'

'Right?' she said.

'Look,' said Callan. 'Just now we run BC Electronics from three places: Roger's flat – but that's full up, only computers need apply – here, and Eaton Square.'

Ellie said, awed, 'You've got a flat in Eaton Square?' Mum was right. This was vast.

'BC has,' said Callan. 'More like a house. Lovely. Only it's a bit small.'

'Small?' Ellie said. '*Eaton Square?*'

'Next year we're due for a visit from a president. *The* President,' Callan said. 'It would be your mum's job to find him a stately home. Yours too, if you want in. Near London. Near a golf course. A place he can relax in – and there'd be other VIP's too.' He turned to Fiona. 'You'd have to organize staff as well. But I'd like Esteban and Emilio to be with us wherever we go.'

'Of course,' Fiona said, and Ellie thought, Oh my God, she means it. She really thinks she can do it, even if she's— She bit off the thought, but this was a word she couldn't swallow. Mad, she thought. From time to time, Mum's crazy, but I adore her. And the major's mad too, but I've started adoring him. But then, for what these two are after, maybe you have to be mad.

'—the apartment in Manhattan and that's it,' Callan was saying. 'Anywhere else, we'll take a suite.'

'You still haven't explained why it isn't a bribe,' Fiona said.

'How can it be?' said Callan. 'A bribe means it's yours to keep – but you don't want that . . . You want to work in the factory. Like me. Like Rog. So work there. It may be mink-lined, but it's still a factory.'

'And you want it all by next week, I suppose?' Fiona said.

'*Next week?*' Callan was appalled. 'As long as it takes, love. Half a lifetime should do it.' He finished his Scotch. 'One more thing. Work clothes . . . Jean Muir, Armani, Cartier. That lot. Now – get it clear, the pair of you. They belong to the company. What you do is wear them and that's it . . . Oh, it'll be rough, I see that. All that silk and satin and sable and mink, but you're a tough pair of biddies. You'll survive.'

'You keep saying *we . . . us . . .*' said Ellie. 'You really want me in it too?'

'Up to you,' said Callan. 'But your mum and me – we're a pair, God help us, only she's got you and I've always fancied a daughter – but who else would take me on? What d'you say?'

'Well, of course,' said Ellie, and kissed him.

'You mean it? You'd do it?' her mother said. 'You'd really do it? Deliver yourself into the hands of that mad ape?' Then, before Ellie could answer, she hugged her and said, 'And why not? It's what I did, after all.'

She put her arms round both of them, then looked up at Callan. 'What a cunning old clever clogs you are,' she said. 'All that loot and none of it mine – it's perfect. I own nothing, therefore, I own everything. Is that it?'

'Bull's eye, Private Wilton,' he said.

'Game of soldiers,' she said. 'Just what I need. Never mind the uniform. Just a quickie, Major . . . Please?'

Callan turned to face his one and only, and Ellie moved into the background. She only played soldiers with her captain.

'B Company' – Callan's voice was a sergeant's effortless roar – 'Get fell in there. Move it! Move it!'

Fiona snapped to attention.

'Let's see how smart you are. Straight and tall, shoulders back.'

'You always enjoy the shoulders back bit,' Fiona said.

'Who wouldn't?' said Callan. 'Now then . . . Orders of the day. Private Wilton will organize the family meal at the hacienda. Dress informal but very, very smart. So, you can go away and change, Private Wilton, and stop poncing about like a refugee from a Turkish brothel.'

'How do you know how—' Fiona began.

'Quiet!' That one word could have cracked a window at Harrods, Ellie thought.

'You've got fifteen minutes, Private Wilton,' said Callan, 'then report to me here. Now then. At the double . . . *march.* Left right, left right, left right, left right . . .'

And her mother doubled to her bedroom, mild as milk. That won't last, Ellie thought, and looked at Callan mopping his forehead.

'Rough, eh?' she said.

'The Falls Road,' said Callan. 'South Armagh, Goose Green, Iraq. Nicks, English and foreign. Your poor old stepdad thought he'd seen it all . . . Till he met your mum.'

'She can be murder, all right,' said Ellie, not without pride.

Callan looked at her. 'You don't *have* to be on the team,' he said. 'We'd still take care of you.'

'I've got to be on the team,' Ellie said. 'It's where all the fun is.'

She went to stand beside her – what did he call himself? Stepdad? – and watched a yacht in the bay.

'Will we have one like that?' she asked him.

'Roger will,' said Callan. 'Only bigger. That one's a bit small for Esteban. *And* your mum.'

Ellie went to change and he brooded on yachts, ships . . . Worst fights there were, in Wellington's day. Cutlass, pistols, get in close. Bang bang, then over the side. Nasty . . .

'Is this all right?' Fiona said, and he turned and gasped aloud. White silk shirt, sapphire-blue trousers that exactly matched her sapphire bracelet, a Basque beret pushed back on her head in a way that was distinctive, witty and completely Fiona.

'I don't know what I've done to deserve this—' he began.

'Oh, but you do,' she said. 'You went to hell.'

'And now it's paradise.'

'Ellie, darling, do be quick,' her mother yelled. 'Your wicked stepfather's going all romantic on me and there just isn't time.'

Nine

The hotel lounge was packed – well, say fifty or so – and the applause began as soon as she appeared, Ellie and darling David two steps behind. Her PA and her minder. Autographs and snapshots and blowing kisses, and the applause like music. Well – maybe some of it was for Melissa. Dressed like a maid in a French farce, that girl was *lethal*. Again Callan mopped his forehead.

'Are you alright?' she asked.

'Fine,' he said, 'but now we're going to *have* to make the ruddy movie.'

For the life or her, she didn't know whether he meant it or not. Ten points to you, O Mighty One. But just you wait, Major darling. Just you wait . . .

The Lagonda snarled and raved its way back to the hut that she now called home. Long, cool rooms, and lazy-swirling fans, while outside, the sun raved worse than the Lagonda. But outside was where they ate: shady trees, the sound of the pool, and roses everywhere. There were even a couple of labradors with pedigrees far, far longer than mine, she thought. Even so, mingle, Fiona. Mingle. You're the hostess, after all. Another marvel, but that one would keep. She would gloat later.

Callan was alone, delighting in what he saw: pretty girls, elegant young men, the two fiesta guitarists playing as if happiness was for ever, and Ellie, Carmencita, Melissa would always be there, and John, William, Angel always glad of it. Then Ellie joined him, and Callan signalled to one of Esteban's minions. Esteban himself was deep in conversation with Fiona.

102

'Getting to know each other?' said Ellie. 'Forget it . . . Getting to know who's boss.'

Callan chuckled. 'He'll soon learn,' he said.

Fiona and Esteban talked of food.

'Quite simple, My Lady,' Esteban was saying. 'Shrimps in a chilli and garlic sauce, grilled swordfish, baby pig . . . and fruit. Our own, of course.'

'Of course,' Fiona said.

'And to drink: champagne—'

'Anything but the FD label,' said Fiona, and Esteban bowed.

'Diamante and our own Rioja. Simple, as I say, My Lady. I regret there was no time to consult you.'

'Not to worry,' said Fiona. 'Not this time. It will give me the chance to see how you and Emilio work together.'

Esteban bowed warily. 'Just so, My Lady . . . *My Lady* is the correct way to speak to you?'

'My Lady will do very well,' Fiona said.

Now the guitars were sad, moody. And quite right too, Callan thought. They're reminding me that nothing lasts. 'When did I know? Really know,' he said aloud. 'Is that it?'

Ellie nodded.

'Guy Fawkes Night,' he said. 'The night she saved my sanity. Some of it, anyway. Even my life.'

They moved to garden chairs, and sat as another minion brought more cava, and Callan relished his kingdom, roses and music and laughter, and even in the Lagonda it was a long way from Potsdam.

'We saw each other every chance we got,' Callan said. 'Dr Rabin reckoned we were good for each other. When one was down, the other was up. But sooner or later we were together. Helping. Caring. We *knew* each other. Like twins.'

Ellie said, 'No . . . love, you mean?'

'Nothing but love,' said Callan. 'It filled the room. No sex. Don't ask me how, but if there'd been sex, I'd have killed for her. Not just an enemy. I'd do that anyway. Do it now. But to be alone again . . .'

103

He looked at her – bewildered, anxious, still – and she looked at his hands. They'd done their share of killing.

'Go on, please,' she said.

'But Bonfire Night was too much. Volcanoes and Catherine wheels and big bangs and little bangs. Bonfires and music on the telly. José Feliciano, "Light My Fire". And Zippos. Bloody Zippos. It was the only word I could say. At first she thought it was rude. Like the family jewels. Soldier's talk. It fascinated her.'

'What is it really?'

'Cigarette lighter. A man I knew used to play with one. Like a toy.'

'I think I knew him too.'

'He's not well,' said Callan. 'The thing is, he doesn't know it . . .'

He read the signs on her face and said, 'Not for you. Not even for your mum . . . For me. I owe him, love. Where was I?'

'The bonfire.'

'They lit it, and Guy Fawkes burned and they all cheered. It was too much. The flames burned all over him – licked his face like they were a bloody dog and I said, "That Voss. *He* did that . . ." and off I went to kill him – only, your mum cracked me over the head with a vase – she's murder on vases, your mum – and I had a bit of a lie down instead, and when I came to, she was laughing and crying together like she does and she said—'

Behind him, Fiona said softly, 'Wait till after the bonfire, when it's dark. *Then* you can kill him and we'll be happy.'

He turned to face her and smiled, and Ellie thought, Oh, please God. Make John smile at me like that. Just once.

'You're the boss,' her mother continued. 'That's what you said, then you picked me up and I floated like a leaf . . . So gently. Like a leaf in the breeze, and we lay on the sofa, still as statues, till you fell asleep and I had to go back.'

'Go back where?' Ellie asked.

'Bayswater. Your father was trying to sell what we had left to give it to your husband. So I went back and there was George, rampaging in the kitchen.'

'Rampaging?' said Ellie.

'Doing his best, anyway,' Fiona said. 'Which isn't saying much – I'm sorry, darling, but he really was awful. Almost as awful as me.'

Ellie got up and put her arms round Fiona. 'Finish it, Mum,' she said.

'He wasn't quite sure how to make a cup of tea,' Fiona said. 'I was worried sick because I might never see David again and this oaf was wittering on about how to boil a kettle.'

'He really couldn't make tea?' Ellie asked.

'There were times when he couldn't make water,' Fiona said.

There was a shout from the end of the garden. Two wooden tables for a stage, and Carmencita was dancing. Callan got up and walked towards her and Fiona smiled.

'You asked him?' she said.

'About that night? I had to, Mum. It changed you so much. What a pair . . . You put him back together and he did the same for you. What a team.'

Callan joined Mars and together they watched Carmencita. She was a sight worth watching. Green this time, and white polka dots that swirled as she danced. Snow in summer. As they watched, Esteban, stately as a cardinal, walked up to Fiona. Pope Joan, thought Mars.

'Look at him,' said Callan. 'All calm and dignified. He doesn't even know he's in chains and Fiona's got the only key.'

Carmencita danced on with the same wild elegance. Angel's hands clapped like rifle fire as Fiona joined them.

'She's cured, then?' she asked, and when Callan nodded, she sighed in relief.

'She's going with us to Seville tomorrow,' and Callan smiled.

'Fine,' he said.

'Shouldn't we go too?' William asked.

'You'd look ridiculous in a skirt,' said Fiona. 'Gorgeous – but ridiculous.' She patted his cheek.

Callan turned to Melissa. 'You're going?'

'All those dress shops?' Melissa said. 'Try and stop me.'

105

'Fine,' said Callan. The dance ended, the guests applauded, and Esteban came up to Fiona and said, 'Lunch is served, My Lady.'

Two by two, the guests went in, and the guitarists played a different tune: still very Spanish, but stately, elegant. For a moment, Fiona stood and listened, serious, sad even, then took Callan by the arm and they went in to lunch.

In their bedroom, Fiona relaxed, while Callan dried himself after a shower.

'I *think* he likes me,' she said.

'He adores you,' said Callan.

'And you're right. He *is* as big a snob as you are.'

'You want me to give it up?'

'Certainly not,' she said. 'Come here.'

He lay beside her.

'Melissa.'

'What about her?'

'She's on our team, isn't she? *Fine*, you said.'

'It will be, if she's there,' said Callan. 'Just for now, she's sort of tutoring William.'

'Doesn't John have a tutor?'

'I'm doing that,' Callan said.

'Oh, the poor sweet baa-lamb,' Fiona said, then: 'Ellie.'

'What about her?' he asked.

'Tomorrow,' Fiona said. 'Did you really mean it? Expense no object?'

'Well, of course I mean it.'

'Oh, you *do* know how to get round us middle-aged mums.'

'Not so much of the middle-aged,' said Callan. 'Just make sure she spends. We can afford it.'

She embraced him, kissed him.

'Those are the most beautiful words I ever heard,' she said, and stroked his back, so that he relaxed even more. Then suddenly she froze.

'Oh my God, they're there too,' she said. 'Those bloody lumps.'

'You can see them?' said Callan. 'Dr Kretz said—'

'Feel them. Not like the ones on your chest . . . Under those

106

white lines on your back. Like whip marks.' She turned to face him, eyes staring hard into his. 'They *are* whip marks,' she said. 'Oh, the bastards. Why don't you hit me?'

'You've lost me,' said Callan. 'Why should I hit you?'

'Touching you like that,' she said. 'Were they so bad, those doctors?'

'They were the best,' Callan said. 'I told you. All three of them. All Jews. All Mossad. And they fought death for me like he was an SS man.'

'You were such a hero.' Not a question. A statement.

'To them I was,' said Callan. 'They knew all about the Potsdam Hilton.'

'And all I did was treat you like a bloody freak.'

'We've been into all that. You can touch me any time you like, and I wish you would. Here.'

From beneath the pillow he took the Basque beret, put it on her head.

'Now you're Shiva,' he said. 'Hindu Goddess of love. So, get cracking.'

'*With a hat on*? You mean while we're—'

'You know whatting,' he said. 'Before, during, after. So get to work, Private Wilton. We haven't got all day.'

'Oh yes we have, O Mighty One,' Fiona said. 'We've got all the time in the world.'

The white Merc drove up to the house. On the way, Melissa stared, looked at the vast bonfire, then turned to Hunter.

'Jee-*zuz*,' she said. 'Even the Ku Klux Klan never made one that big.'

'That's a good-guys' bonfire,' said Ellie. 'Let's go and buy some dresses.'

'Yassum, Miss Ellie,' Melissa said.

By the door, Carmencita and Fiona waited, then got into the car. Ellie moved to the back seat, and looked at her mother warily. She limped a little.

'Now what are you up to?' she asked.

'Dancing lessons,' said Fiona. 'Sevillanas, as a matter of fact. Such fun . . . I'm knackered.'

From the front, Carmencita called, '*Ahora? A Sevilla?*'

'*Si*,' they called in chorus.

'*Salimos, Señoritas. Vamanos. Adelante.*'

The Mercedes slid away.

Callan looked down from his veranda as it moved: the most beautiful chauffeur in Spain, most beautiful navigator, far and away the most beautiful passengers. He could think about it all day, but Hunter went and spoiled it. Another thing women were good at . . . She and Gerald were on the veranda too, watching as Mars and William appeared in the Morgan and galloped after the Merc.

'Four of them,' Hunter said. 'Poor defenceless little rose-buds. And only two gorillas to protect them, and two more on the road, and two women in the boutique.'

'Don't forget Melissa,' Callan said, and Hunter sighed.

'Who could ever forget Melissa?'

'And Fiona's a dab hand with a shotgun, they tell me. Cups and things,' Gerald said.

'She hasn't brought it with her,' said Hunter, then: 'Oh my God. She hasn't, has she?'

'Time will tell,' said Callan, and then: 'These women at the boutique – they're good?'

'The best,' said Hunter. 'Sir said they had to be the best.'

'That'll have to do,' said Callan, and Hunter erupted.

'You've got a nerve!' she said.

'If he didn't, we wouldn't be here,' said Gerald. 'Drawing room?'

Callan nodded and they went into the house, to a big, cool room where Gerald could prowl and examine the pictures, the statues, the odds and sods. At the moment, it was the model of a cannon from Wellington's time. Hunter and Callan sat and enjoyed the fan's swirl, like Carmencita taking it easy, but that was impossible.

'Nerve?' he said. 'I'm gambling my whole family. But that's not nerve. That's crazy. Like me.'

'I'm sorry,' Hunter said.

'No no,' said Callan. 'It's just that if Voss gets his hands on them . . . I'm out.'

'You'd give up?'

'I'd kill him,' said Callan. 'It's what you want anyway. For them too.'

'Ellie?' said Hunter. 'Fiona?'

'This isn't the face Voss gave me,' said Callan. 'No way.'

She looked at him. So cool, so calm, so reasonable – and totally and completely round the twist.

Gerald put down the cannon.

'Much better to wait,' he said. 'Stay with the plan.'

'If I can,' said Callan, 'I will.'

'That'll do me,' Hunter said. 'You're the boss.'

'Don't you believe it,' Callan said and called to Gerald, who was looking at a snarling silver tiger. 'Gerald, my lovely. Who's the boss?'

'Take your pick. MI6 Head of Section, CIA Head of Section, Buck House, the FO, the PM. You. Me. Hunter.'

The tiger continued to snarl and Gerald snarled back.

Hunter was appalled. 'You're saying all that lot know about this?'

'No no,' said Gerald, soothing as cough syrup. 'Bits . . . That's all I've told them. *Need to know* . . . We're the only ones who know the lot.'

'Even so. All those VIPs to kill one man?'

'Two, in fact. Maybe three,' Gerald said. 'Smethwick, of *course*. Naughty books, indeed. They really will be the death of him. And Voss because he's greedy. And Bishop, if we can ever trace him. And all for money. Doubloons, pieces of eight, golden guineas. Like the Mafia. Don't you find it a little squalid, dear boy?'

'Better than a Zippo lighter,' said Callan, and brooded. 'If only it wasn't such a mess,' he said. 'You in charge. Fine. Or Hunter here. Or even me.'

'You're climbing fast, Callan,' Hunter said. 'From Hunter's scrapyard to Buck House in one leap. How d' you do it?'

Callan grinned at her. 'By owning half of BC Electronics,' he said.

'That must be some laptop you're peddling,' said Hunter. 'MI6, CIA. The odd royal.'

'The extremely odd royal,' said Gerald.

'But if David's so big – why risk him?' Hunter asked.

'His manly looks, you mean? His boyish charm?' said Gerald. 'My dear, if we – the major's team – do the job, then only we know. It's that damn book, of course.'

'But David swiped that,' said Hunter.

'To be sure – and very nice too.' Gerald beamed at them. 'But there were notes, rough drafts—'

'Well, of course,' said Hunter, 'but—'

'Rather more than we'd realized. Computer transcripts.'

'Hot stuff?' said Hunter.

'Incandescent,' said Gerald. 'Letters, tapes. The *things* those young people were up to. One wonders if Daddy had the remotest idea—'

'Daddy?' Hunter queried.

'Prince, president, sultan,' said Gerald. 'No wonder they send their naughty boys here.'

'I'm sorry, I—'

'We care for them,' said Callan, 'in a nick like the Savoy. Four square methadones a day.'

'Just like Smacker,' Hunter said.

'Not unless you fancy a war,' said Callan.

'Smethwick's enough,' said Gerald. 'He doesn't like David at all. Wants to arrange his funeral.'

Hunter knew all about death. She'd been there often enough. But these two made it sound like a game of ludo.

'D' you think he can?' she asked.

'He's good – with a shotgun, maybe the best. But he's on his own. No back-up.'

'What about Señor what's his name – Mendez?'

'Last seen in the dustbin, would you say? *Basura*,' said Callan.

'You mean, he's crazy?'

'I mean, he's dead,' said Callan. Hunter began to understand why Betty had felt such an overwhelming need for Scotch.

'He and his friends are no longer with us,' said Gerald. 'Motorbikes and skips and things. A garbage truck their last resting place.'

'Dust to dust,' said Callan.

'They've disappeared, it seems,' said Gerald.

'The piledriver would have been better,' said Callan, and Hunter jumped as if he'd hit her.

'I've got my own scrapyard now,' he said. '*And* a piledriver. Works a treat.'

'That must be nice for you,' she said.

'Like you've no idea.'

'In a moment,' said Gerald. 'Let's get Pancho out of the way.' He sighed. 'If only one could.'

Ten

The Mercedes ate the Seville road like spaghetti. Behind it the Morgan followed respectfully. It knew its place. Nice to take a drive with John, thought Ellie. Just as soon as he gets a Mercedes. Beside her, mum began to sing, and so did she.

> Why am I always the bridesmaid,
> Never the blooming bride?
> Ding dong, wedding bells
> Always ring for other gels . . .

From a side road, a Jaguar cut in ahead of the Morgan, and at once Melissa accelerated, smooth, relaxed, pushing the speed to 200 kph. The Mercedes didn't mind a bit. The Jaguar did. Two hundred kph wasn't a problem, but its driver was.

Last in the procession, Mars all but stood on the Morgan's accelerator and yelled to William, 'This is no way to visit a boutique.'

William closed his eyes.

Suddenly Melissa eased off and turned right, no signals, no warning, into a restaurant car park. The Jaguar almost lost her, turned just in time. Driver and passenger reached for their doors, then suddenly the Morgan's horn blasted, Gabriel on Judgement Day, and screeched to a stop between the two big cars. William leaped out, running wide of the Jaguar, whose driver appeared to have a handgun – and so, like a conjuring trick, did William.

'Hands on your head!' he said.

'Now look here—' the driver said.

'On your head, boss,' said William. It was the last word that did it. The driver obeyed. His passenger already had. 'This is a Smith and Wesson .357 magnum with a three-and-a-half

112

inch barrel, chequered walnut stock, satin-blue finish,' said William. 'At this range, it's very, very accurate, and we both want you to be nice. Will you – just to oblige us?'

'Oh, yes,' said the passenger. 'Of course we'll be nice.'

The driver didn't seem so sure, till William aimed the magnum at his forehead. And even then he was silent. Guts? Mars wondered. Stupidity? A bowel problem? William released the S and W's safety catch and the tiny metallic click was the loudest sound in the world. The driver got out.

'I say, what fun,' Fiona said.

Carmencita lifted her sunglasses. 'William – he's kill him?'

'Not beside my car,' Melissa said firmly. 'Blood's murder to get off.'

'We're hungry.' said Ellie.

'Eat, then,' said Mars. 'Only, leave the Merc in the shade.'

Melissa drove off, the other three blew kisses, and Mars and William put up their guns. William smiled at the driver.

'I'm going to ask you questions,' he said. 'Best thing you can do is answer. Right, John?'

'Oh, absolutely,' said Mars. 'It's far too hot for the rough work.'

William grasped the driver's coat, lifted him as he would a five-year-old.

'Let's hear it, boss,' he said.

Mars went to the Morgan and took out the mobile . . .

'Pancho?' said Callan.

Gerald looked furtive.

'The – er – *muchacho* at the fiesta. And his – mate, would it be? Smith or Robinson or Cholmondely Davenport – something like that.' He looked at Hunter.

'Police fast-track whizz-kid,' she said. 'He's working with the section for field experience.'

'Any good?' Callan asked.

There was a long silence. When the phone rang she and Gerald looked relieved as Callan answered.

'John,' Callan said. 'Are you all OK? Good. Good . . . *Who*? But nobody told— Stupid what? Oh. Imbecile. Put the mate in the Jag – he seems to have some sense – then tell William to duff the driver. Not you . . . you hit too hard. When he cries, take his picture. Then get back here. You're what? Hungry? You're always hungry. Get Emilio to make you a sandwich. And John . . . Nice one. Tell William I said so.'

He hung up and stared long and hard at Gerald.

'And I thought you were a mate,' he said.

'David,' Gerald said. 'I know it sounds bad—'

'It stinks,' said Callan.

'We had no *choice*,' said Hunter.

Callan rose. 'Let yourselves out,' he said.

'You can't leave,' said Gerald. 'Believe me.'

'You're going to shoot me? Want me to turn my back?'

'Oh, dear God,' Gerald said. And then: 'David, believe me. That's the order. All the way to the top. If you do, Roger—'

'Don't be stupid,' said Callan. 'He's the goose that lays the golden eggs.'

'Hostage,' said Gerald. 'So long as you're nice, he'll be fine.'

'You haven't got a Zippo lighter I could borrow?' Callan asked.

Hunter said, 'It was my idea. I hadn't talked to you then . . . but even if I had . . . it was orders. Accept it, Callan. What's locked up in your friend's skull is worth billions.'

'I could try the Israelis,' Callan said, 'but they can't afford me. Or I could kill the pair of you, now Pancho the Peril's out of the way. I could do that, couldn't I, Hunter?'

She looked at him steadily. 'Of course you could.'

'But I'd have to drive you to the scrapyard, tie you to the bedding plate. It's tricky, that bedding plate, Gerald. The first smack sometimes spreads a bit. I could break your necks, of course, but where's the fun in that?'

'That's enough,' said Gerald.

'No, it isn't,' said Callan. 'I'm gambling my life.' He shrugged. 'No big deal. I've been doing it for years. But I'm also gambling the lives of all the people I love. And who's going to take over? Pancho? The guy who follows four good-looking birds in a Merc because it's just what he always wanted – and he loves it so much he even forgets to report in first.'

Callan mimed a man thinking hard. Rodin's *Le Penseur* with clothes on, then suddenly he smiled.

'Well, of course,' he said. 'That's it. I mean, here we are worrying ourselves sick, and all the time it's staring us in the face – I'll join the CIA.'

'But you can't,' said Gerald.

'Course I can,' said Callan. 'I phone their red number and that's it. Roger and Fiona and me. Citizens of that great republic –' he put his hand to his heart as if the band already played. *Oh, say can you see?* 'Then off to Manhattan with enough bodyguards to start a war. And they would too, if I asked them nicely.'

'You set this up, didn't you?' said Hunter.

'Just like you set up Pancho.'

'Bishop set up Pancho. He – knows things. Drug busts and things. He's in, so he can't be moved. Like a fossil in stone.'

'Lose him, then.'

'He *wants* to be a spy. That makes him an idiot, but it's what he wants.'

'Kill him, then.'

She looked at him: calm, relaxed, marvellous tan, and grey eyes that told no more than puddles in the rain.

'Should be a pushover,' said Callan. 'Silly sod even thinks he's tough. They're always the easy ones.'

Again she looked at him: the probing look that for once did her no good at all.

At last he said, 'You've just remembered something. Want to tell us what it is?'

She shook her head, not daring to speak. He was the cat now. Mice stayed quiet.

'You've remembered I'm crazy,' he said.

The procession swept up to the hacienda forecourt. This time the Morgan led, the Jaguar followed, William driving, Pancho's oppo beside him.

'I'm afraid this is it,' William said. 'We can call a taxi for you.'

'Be a help,' said the other. Jones, was it? Robinson? *Brown.* That was it, DI Brown. A bit lost, but really rather nice.

'Do you want to collect Pancho first?'

'*No*!' Brown, it seemed, was utterly certain. 'If you don't mind . . .'

Mars got out and joined them. 'We'll see,' he said.

'You could say you dropped me at the hotel. Told the driver where to take me. Make on I don't speak Spanish.'

'You do?'

'I can get by,' said Brown.

'And Pancho?' Mars asked.

'Not a word,' said Brown. 'Six months notice we were coming here, and not a bleeding word.'

No doubt about it, thought Mars. He'd earned his smacks from William.

Callan pressed a button and the curtains closed. All present. The two he'd have to think about and John and William and a vast plate of sandwiches. Callan pressed another button and helped himself to a sandwich as the screen glowed, the film began. Oast houses, hops, downland, and about a million sheep. The manor house now a golf club, a glimpse of a smooth and easy sea. Two men with dogs – a retriever and a big spaniel. Smethwick and his loader, Smethwick in tweed cap, Barbour jacket, boots. Not like a lawyer at all, and the loader carrying the second gun, as Kentish as the soil they stood on.

And then they came, the long untidy line of pheasant, and the two men became frantically busy: fire, swap guns, load, fire, swap guns, and the birds tumbled out of the sky; the shotguns blazed, fast and accurate, so that at one point five birds dived to the earth like kamikazes. 'Jesus!' said Mars. Callan bit into another sandwich.

Cut then to a man running hard across the downland, and in the distance, the sweetly melancholy cry of hounds moving up to the kill. Then the camera cut to them. Beagles. With that build, they shouldn't be able to run at all, but they could run all right, Callan thought. Far better than the men and women trying to keep up. But then, the beagles didn't smoke.

Then another shot of Smethwick, seated in the shade of a beaten-up old Land Rover, cleaning his guns, and somewhere near, the hounds were in full cry, but Smethwick didn't even look up. His guns were too important . . .

That evening, they gave a party for their daughter's new frocks. Ellie, Melissa, Carmencita, John, William, Angel . . . And Hunter and Gerald. Callan put a jeweller's loupe to his eye, tightened a screw and spun a wheel on the cannon. Then – Suvorov, he thought, Russian general. Probably a prince. In those days, all the winners were princes. And he really did know how to win. Even the French. Even Napoleon . . .

Trouble was, he starved them. Scorched earth. Nothing wrong with starving Frenchmen, but all those noble Russian cavalry wanted action. Like Pancho, he thought. Well, they got it, and of course, Napoleon won. All the same, the Brits gave Suvorov a couple of cannon. Birmingham's best. Long gone. All that was left was the model . . . Lovely thing. The CD player began another tune. George Shearing, 'Let There Be Love'. Nat King Cole the singer. Long gone . . . When's your turn, Callan? No rush. He had to get her well first.

A book landed in his lap: a hard, heavy book. *The Art of India*. He forced himself not to yell. Fiona said, 'I bought it in Seville. Page eighty-four.' He looked at her: unhappy didn't begin to tell it. Better look at page eighty-four. Vishnu. It would be. Pretty well starkers, except for a hat.

'What's wrong with it?' he asked.

'*Wrong?*'

Fix bayonets and charge, he thought. It was all in the voice.

'Sexy. Beautiful. What's wrong with that? A thousand million Hindus can't be wrong. Pity you can't ask my grandfather.'

'Your grandfather was a Hindu?'

'He was a swaddy,' he said, and she laughed. No bayonet charge.

'Don't you ever lose?' she said, then: 'Do you still want me to go to London on Thursday?'

'Friday,' he said.

'Time to wash the blood off the carpet?' she said.

'They have a machine does that nowadays.'

117

He looked at Ellie, laughing in Mars's arms. 'Tell me your thoughts, O Bluebeard,' Fiona said.

'Ellie . . .' He looked at her again. No jeans. No workshops. Gown and jewels just about perfect. 'You did us proud,' he said.

'Oh, you.' She watched the dancers. 'They've got a lot to learn about dancing, the pair of them. Let's show them.' Tommy Dorsey, 'Sunny Side of the Street'. 'Come on.'

She grabbed his hand and dragged him to the music. She looked younger than Ellie, but she danced better.

'About this London trip,' she said. 'I thought I might drop in on some of my nastier relatives. Aunt Griselda, say. She'll be at her country place.'

'Any particular reason?' he asked.

'Make 'em suffer.'

'Nothing wrong with that,' said Callan.

'Oh, dear God, I love you to bits,' she said.

Angel went to the dimmer, lowered the lights, and she moved in closer. 'Is that how they did it at the Hammersmith Palais?'

'Put your arms round my neck,' he said, and she did, and he embraced her.

'That's how they did it at the Hammersmith Palais,' he said.

'But it's gorgeous.'

And so it was, but the words broke the spell, and a bunch of tone-deaf apes called Bang to Rights started to make noises like cars crashing, and they went for a drink instead, and so – surprise, surprise – did Gerald.

'If I might have just the tiniest word.'

'Long as you like,' Callan said, and Gerald looked at Fiona.

'Fiona stays,' said Callan, and Gerald scowled. The Mighty One is causing pain, she thought. What a good idea. Then Hunter came up, far from happy, knowing she was about to get her share.

'Quick as you can, Gerald,' Callan said, but before he could speak, Fiona cut in.

'Phoebe!' she said. 'How scrumptious to see you.' Then

the air kiss, the non-event, and the pretty embarrassment that *always* worked. 'But you're not, are you? Phoebe, I mean. The thing is, you remind me of a girl I knew at the Cordon Bleu School. A sweetie, of *course*, but with rather a problem. Did she like chaps or did she like dolly birds – and all the time she liked both. She was—' she looked at Callan – 'What's the word, sweetness?'

'Rosy,' said Callan, and looked at her fondly, the physics master whose pupil has demonstrated Archimedes' principle without a hitch.

'Actually the lady's name is Charlotte,' he said, 'but I see what you mean.' Like hell I do, he thought, but every little helps, as the old lady said.

'I realize it's all rather complicated,' said Gerald.

'Not complicated at all,' Callan said. 'Yes or no—'

'If you'd sooner you and I talked later . . .'

'Not possible,' said Callan. 'It isn't me on this one. It's the firm.' He put down his empty glass. 'The answer's yes,' he said, 'but it'll cost you. You can bet your pension on that.'

The apes were back in the cage, and Artie Shaw played 'Stardust'.

'Must fly,' he said. 'Do keep in touch.'

Hunter and Gerald joined the dance. All things considered, Fiona thought, they danced rather well.

In the War Room, Callan had resumed work on the cannon. Even five minutes helped. Then Fiona appeared, silk dressing gown, picture of Vishnu, and a yawn.

'My goodness,' she said. 'Such elegance.'

Callan looked in the mirror: lightweight suit, Para tie. 'I'm in disguise,' he said.

'You're not after even more dosh?'

'More like hanging on to what we've got.'

'Being rich,' she said. 'It's disgusting. I like it.'

Then the door bell rang. Once, then again.

'Where's our army of servants?' she asked.

'Church,' said Callan. 'It's Sunday.'

And again the door bell sounded. Fiona went to the door.

119

'I'll go,' she said, and silently he began to count. He'd reached nine when Fiona screamed, then rushed in.

'Something wrong, my dear?' How concerned he was. How grave.

'It's A— A—' she said. 'It's Alf—'

'Alf Higgins? Used to be in C Company? What the devil's he playing at? Ringing bells . . . Frightening the women . . . Don't worry.' He took a sabre from the pattern of arms. 'I'll protect you. Just give me five minutes and I'll run him through.' He flourished the sabre, thrust and cut like Cyrano, and went out. She followed warily to where Callan was looking at a gleaming new Alfa Romeo.

'Oh, that Alf,' he said. 'I must say, she's a dam sight prettier than poor old Higgins.'

'You never give up, do you?' said Fiona. 'I suppose the bloody company bought the car, too.'

'We're far too rich to be a one-car family,' said Callan.

'Then what about my poor Ellie?' said Fiona.

'I thought a Morgan,' said Callan. 'Keep John in the black.'

Wearily she said, 'A Morgan's fine.' Then the rage returned.

'Don't try to change the subject, you bastard,' she said. 'You're at it again. Giving.'

'Just think for a moment, cloth head,' said Callan. 'Soon you'll be in every magazine in Europe – from *Vogue* to *Hello*. And what's your car going to be? A second-hand Lada? Your public will love it.'

'I haven't got a public.'

'You will soon – but not in a Lada. And anyway—'

'What now?' she said.

'I was hoping you'd give me a lift to the airport.'

'Oh, you!' she said.

Eleven

Dogs barked happily, looking forward to their treat, he thought. No, not dogs. Hounds. Must get it right or Naomi would despise him, and that would never do. Looked a treat, Naomi. Dressed for beagling, long and elegant jacket, black velvet cap like a bloody judge when they said, *Hanged by the neck until you are dead* – and meant it. And him beside her. Country tweeds, walking boots, game bag on his shoulder, moving with the mile-eating walk he'd used for so long. Yomping. Not pretty, not ugly, just that steady slog till the man said you could stop. Or, in this case, madam, who seemed delighted to stop, but then, everything in life must be paid for – especially Martinis. Even so, this wouldn't do at all.

'Here?' he said. 'This is asking for it.'

'If you'll just listen . . .' she said.

But he didn't want to listen. He wanted to kill her.

'*He* decided to come here,' she said. 'Not me.'

'And you couldn't move him three miles? Come on.'

Nearby, the beagles barked, the hunters began to assemble, William among them. Right sort of coat, right sort of cap.

'And, God knows, you brought enough witnesses. Did you tell Hunter?'

'No,' she said, 'but—'

'That's all I bloody need,' he said.

'Avram said—'

'Bugger Avram. Stick him,' said Callan. 'This is my party – he hasn't been invited. No way.'

'It's only a mile or two,' she said.

'Three. And cover all the way. For the other bloke.'

'It's a rotten road, anyway,' she said.

121

'For God's sake,' Callan said. 'We're after a four by four. Three miles playing hide and seek with the best twelve-bore shot in the country.'

'I still don't see—'

'Belt up, will you? Just belt up.' He looked away, and called out, 'Nevvy! Come for a spot of exercise?'

Reinforcements. A trump card. Maybe the ace.

'Uncle,' Mars called. 'Good to see you.' Tweeds, flat cap, the right kind of boots. Squire Mars. 'You know William's here?'

Callan looked at William, knee deep in beagles. 'One big happy family,' he said. 'You've met Mrs Nettles?'

'Ms Klein,' she said.

'She's our guide,' said Callan.

'A bit lost for a guide, surely?' said Mars.

'She does get lost from time to time,' said Callan. 'But three miles is neither here nor there. She told me so herself.'

'Did she, now?' said Mars. 'She looks tired.'

'Maybe it's the handbag,' said Callan. 'A bit heavy for such an elegant lady.'

No signal, no warning, but Mars's left hand grabbed her arm, and, of course, she struggled, and pain scalded her wrist, her hand opened, and she let her handbag fall.

'Odd, that,' said Mars. 'A handbag out hunting. Mean to say – she's got pockets in places you and—'

'Nevvy, that will do,' Callan said, then to Ms Klein: 'You'll have to excuse him. Impressionable lad. It isn't often he gets so close to a lady . . .' And then to Mars: 'Better have a look, Nevvy.'

Make-up, credit cards, money – lots of it – comb, driving licence – all perfectly normal. But the gun wasn't. A work of art, or at least of craft.

'Colt Woodsman,' Mars said. 'A bit antique, but it's in good nick. She's being naughty, Uncle David.'

'Oh dear, oh dear,' said Callan. 'Naughty ladies. What's the world coming to?'

'We all have our dreams, Uncle.' He extracted the Colt's magazine.

'Give it back?'

'Why not?' said Callan. 'Slow her down a bit.' He looked at his watch. 'Fancy a look at the bad guy? Top of that hillock thing there. Eleven o'clock.'

Mars went to the downland's crest and looked the way he had been taught. The little Jap field glasses showed it all. Land Rover, Smethwick cleaning his shotgun, springer spaniel glad of a rest.

The beagle pack began yelping as one, like a choir that still has a lot to learn. William seemed to be festooned in them.

'Oh, I say,' said Callan. 'Tally-ho, and all that sort of rot.'

'Do we go with them?' Naomi Klein asked. Not happy. Not at all happy. Nor should she be . . . Mars slid silently down the grass and joined them.

'What d' you think, Nevvy?' he asked. 'Our chum's going to join a Zippo collector. What they call a deal. Money-for-goods kind of thing. Straightforward stuff, but it *is* three miles. And we'd have to walk it. Start now.'

'It's a bit of a hike, Uncle,' Mars said.

Callan turned to Naomi. 'It's the damp weather,' he said. 'His croquet leg, you know. Shocking business. Ruined his game. Last week he caught a bishop with his follow through.'

He waited for a reaction to the word bishop. Zilch. Either a good actress or she hadn't been told.

'It baffles me where a man of God could learn words like that,' said Mars.

Callan appeared to be meditating on bishops, parsons, deacons, even vergers, but what he said was, 'Do it here.'

'Here?' She was appalled. Suppose he missed, or the beagles bit him. *Suppose Smethwick saw who she was?*

'We have to consider my nephew's leg. I know the bishop did. But it's perfectly simple.'

'You think so, Uncle?'

'Nothing to it,' said Callan. 'We attract our friend's attention – you could show him your leg – help him to a better world – then, hey ho, back to town just in time for drinkies . . .'

'Spot on,' said Mars. 'Just one thing. Why can't we show him Ms Klein's leg?'

'Nevvy,' said Callan. 'That's a perfectly marvellous idea. He's probably never glimpsed a female leg like that before, and now there she is. The last thing he sees before he leaves this vale of tears.' Solemnly he removed his cap.

'Instead of a hearty breakfast you mean.'

Callan was reproachful. 'Nevvy, that's not nice,' he said. 'Ms Klein has very nice legs.' Mars turned to her.

'Listen to me,' Naomi Klein said.

Her hands were shaking. Interesting, that. Melissa's hands didn't shake . . .

'If you don't stop this, I'll scream,' she said.

'And, if you scream, I'll belt you,' said Callan, talking at last like Roger's mate.

'You'd do better showing His Nibs your leg,' said Mars.

'Brains,' said Callan. 'Up here.' He tapped his forehead. 'That's where you need it. Hot stuff, my nephew. Very hot. You know anything about heat, Ms Klein?'

Oh God, she thought. Why did Avram have to tell me?

'Hot stuff hurts, you see,' said Callan. 'Hurts like hell sometimes. Flame and red-hot coals and the devils all wearing asbestos underwear. But you're not.'

He was looking at a blackbird, perched on a bush in flower.

We're off again, Mars thought. The clean pure line of the bird's melody, Glory to God. But it won't reach down to hell.

At last Callan said. 'You brought that car that climbs trees?'

Mars nodded.

'Bring it closer in, would you?'

Mars took off and they waited until at last the hunting horn sounded, and the beagles yelped. The whole hunt moved, led by a black man who was impeccable, even beautiful, but it was all madness. Men and women and hounds streamed past and they tagged on at the end, and Mars joined them, ran by her side, and Callan dropped back behind her. Nice, very nice, she thought. Whatever I do, they'll kill me before I go five yards.

The ruined railway culvert then, so soon, and the Land Rover close by; Smethwick watching, shotgun under his arm. The black man ran into the culvert, and the beagles followed, all merry and bright as if school was out, she thought. Mine isn't.

Into the half-light of the culvert, the sour smell of rotting brick. Callan's hand reached out and she stopped. Mars took over and they followed Callan to the culvert's mouth. *He was carrying a gun* – and she hadn't even seen where it came from. He moved towards the sunlight, and the spaniel still sleeping, Smethwick with his back to them, going to the four by four. Callan eased the safety catch on the gun – a revolver; OK Corral stuff – and stepped into the light as the spaniel woke, yawned, then began to bark. At once, Smethwick snapped the shotgun together, and Callan called, 'Oi, Smethy,' and Smethwick whirled, the shotgun halfway to his shoulder when Callan killed him.

Textbook stuff, Mars thought. Heart and head, and down he goes. 'What'll it be sir – a goldfish or a cigar?'

She ran into the sunlight. They always do, the new ones, the trainees, the novices. Then they try to hide. Just as she was doing; wriggling into the ground behind a stone no bigger than her head.

'What now?' he asked.

Callan shrugged and called to the woman, 'On your feet. There's a good girl.'

Slowly, reluctantly, Ms Klein emerged from under her stone. 'I feel sick,' she said.

'Not till I say so,' said Callan. 'You stay there where we can see you. We don't want you getting lost again.'

He looked at her. She really did feel sick, he thought. There was a loo in the Eaton Square house that colour. He didn't like it.

'Your first time, was it?' he asked. 'Virgin, were we?' She nodded. 'You'll get used to it.'

'Dear God,' she said.

Avram *must* be short-handed, he thought. To send a – what? Novice? Intern? On a caper like this.

'Now then,' he said, and looked in her handbag, took out an *Evening Standard* and turned to Mars.

'Blood, would you say? Spot of gore?'

Mars took a plastic-wrapped syringe from his pocket. 'Be a brave girl,' he said. 'We only want a smidgen.'

He grabbed Naomi, held her so that she couldn't move, and used the syringe, while Callan watched sleepily.

'On the paper,' he said, and Mars dribbled a little blood on the newspaper.

'There,' he said. 'That wasn't so bad, was it?' then went to help Callan heave Smethwick's body into the driving seat, and the blackbird came back to the bush and sang to the good guys. Callan got up into the Land Rover, now a makeshift hearse.

'Poor chap,' he said. 'He never saw her legs,' and reversed into the culvert.

The blackbird sang some coloratura stuff and Mars said, 'You don't do Mozart by any chance?' But the blackbird took no notice.

'Temperamental,' said Mars. 'Just because they—'

'He killed him,' she said. 'You're an accessory.'

'What are you going to do? Arrest us?'

Again, she interrupted him. 'That makes me an accessory too.'

'You're alive, Mrs Thing. At least you are till Uncle David says otherwise.'

This time she didn't interrupt: she just legged it. They really were nice legs, but even so – he took off after her, then brought her down with a rugger tackle.

She lay there on the grass and looked up at him. Not trying it on. Just – bewildered. How could these terrible things be happening to Naomi Klein?

'You were naughty,' said Mars. 'You didn't bring a pack of cards, I don't suppose?'

Callan came out of the culvert, shotgun in one hand, game bag in the other. He even looks happy, she thought . . . Sunlight and birdsong, a hunting horn, and far away on the crest of the downland, tiny moving figures, dozens of them, and all to kill a hare.

Mars looked at the shotgun. 'Nice,' he said.

'A Churchill,' said Callan. 'I could do with one like this. Mind you, two would have been better.' He sighed. 'There's always something. Now then. Let me put you chaps in the picture. Our friend's in the Land Rover. Engine running. Tube from the exhaust to his seat. Windows stuffed with newspaper. Interesting, wouldn't you say?'

'Fascinating,' said Mars. 'If it's what it looks like, our friend shot himself twice with .357 magnum bullets – yet all his ammo's for a twelve-bore. Then, after he's shot himself – fatally, if I may say so, Uncle—'

'You certainly may,' said Callan.

'After he's *dead*, in fact, he backs the four-wheel drive into the culvert all by himself, seals himself in, and dies of carbon monoxide poisoning, having already died of gunshot wounds. And he hasn't even got a shotgun. Is that it?'

'Blood on the newspaper,' Callan said.

'Sorry, Uncle . . . His body's unmarked, apart from the magnum wounds, and there's blood on the evening paper – and probably not his blood either. You know, Uncle, this beats the *Marie Celeste* any day.'

'Why, thank you, my boy,' said Callan, and turned to Naomi.

'Anything to add?' he asked.

'I feel sick.'

'When I say so,' said Callan. 'Mind you, I see your point. His face *is* a bit of a mess.'

The car that climbed trees was of course a Morgan, and after it had sailed up a hillside with an impossible gradient, Callan began to believe it. At last it reached a road, they drove to where a Volvo was waiting and she got out at once. Leaving us, and glad to do it, he thought. Even her colour had improved.

'See you later, Mrs Whatsit,' he said.

'Not if I can help it,' she said.

'But you can't. You're not the Queen of the County Court now. You're a –' he looked at Mars – 'What was that word?'

'A serf,' said Mars.

'A scullion. A nothing, Mrs Thingy,' said Callan. 'You couldn't even stand the sight of a dead man, which means you're quite nice, really. Next time we meet – just keep out of the way. Innocent bystander, that's you.'

She flounced into the Volvo and drove off.

'You old softy,' said Mars and drove on to a lay-by, where a furniture van waited with its driver, who opened it up at once.

Mars drove the Morgan into it, shut the doors, and they looked at Ms Thing's money. Gerald would be pleased – if they gave him any.

An elegant room, Fiona thought. Smart and yet discreet, just like Uncle Theo, but then, this was Wimpole Street, and Uncle Theo the best doctor for miles. His waiting room had to be elegant. Splodgy modern paintings on the walls, glossies of x-rays on the table. Somebody forgot to clear away, she thought. Somebody's for it. She tucked one of the glossies into a splodgy's frame. Much better.

Then Uncle Theo came in looking like a distinguished doctor in a movie, and gawked. Very gratifying, that gawk. Not just Givenchy and Gucci but the lady who filled them.

'Uncle Theo, how *nice*,' she said.

'Crazy, that's what it is,' he said.

'You should know,' she said. 'You're the doctor.'

She kissed his cheek.

'Why Rabin should decide to be ill this day of all days . . .' he said. 'I've already had a phone call . . .'

'Poor Uncle,' Fiona said, and then: 'Just one? I thought I did rather better than that.'

'Or maybe it was three. Your Aunt Griselda, your cousin Drusilla and your cousin Tristram.'

'Tristram's learned to use the *phone*,' said Fiona. 'How super.'

'Not if you're the one on the other end . . . Have a drink.'

'Have you any red Rioja?'

He looked at her then, not gawking: appraising and yet loving. Nice.

'Like that, is it?' he said. 'No, I haven't any red Rioja. G&T's what I have.' He took drinks from a fridge marked with a skull and crossbones. 'What the devil are you playing at?'

'I popped over to see them.'

'*Popped over?*' Theo said. 'They live in Northumberland.'

'There are such things as helicopters,' said Fiona.

'Ah,' Theo said. 'Chucking our money about, were we?'

'Why not? A bit of it *is* mine. I can chuck it if I want to. Most of it's David's and Roger's, of course, and the rest's R and D. They're a bunch of weirdos called BC Electronics.'

'Weirdos?'

'Computers,' said Fiona. 'David reckons they're all madly in love with Roger. One of them is queer.'

Theo blinked. 'My dear, I know you wouldn't lie to me, but is it relevant?' he said. 'There's the devil of a lot to do.' He lifted his glass. 'Cheers.' And then: 'That's better. Let's hear it.'

'They must have told you I'm rich? Gold-digger and shameless hussy and, *Did you see those sapphires?* All that.'

'But what did you expect?' said Theo.

'What I got . . . What I went for . . . Me in a Givenchy exclusive and Aunt Griz wearing barbed wire next to the skin. They were having coffee.'

'Appalling, no doubt.'

'No coffee for shameless hussies with sapphires, Uncle Theo. Just as well I took my own champers. David owns the vineyard.' She smiled. Innocent, content.

She's still tasting it, he thought. Even the memory, bless her.

'I told them all about it,' she said, 'and the Lagonda and the hacienda and the servants, and the house in Eaton Square. It seems we have a Bentley there. They were absolutely gobsmacked. Such fun . . . Cows, the lot of them. Except for poor old Tristram, of course. He's more a sort of bewildered bullock.'

'Let's talk about your problem,' he said. 'Outside. Get some fresh air.'

'*Fresh air*? Uncle Theo, you hate fresh air.' She looked at him and the smile came back. 'We're being bugged,' she said. 'How super.'

'It's possible,' Theo said. 'Gerald's a nosy old queen, they tell me.' He put a finger to his lips. 'Brisk walk in the park,' he said firmly. 'That's the ticket. Maybe you should buy a dog.'

'I've got a dog,' she said.

'Then get another.' He took her by the elbow. 'Fresh air.'

The Serpentine was busy, but they managed two seats and

watched the children doing their best to drown themselves. Their car had turned every head it passed before it left them to it.

'What on earth is it?' Theo asked.

'1950s Lincoln Continental. It belongs to Roger. He's a film fan. George Raft drove one in a movie on TV. He adores that car. He even bought a fedora hat.'

'He bought a car, too,' Theo said. 'My God, did he.'

'He quite often does,' said Fiona. The chauffeur got out and lit a cigarette.

'Let's stay with your problem,' Theo said.

'David's not a problem,' said Fiona. 'My darling. My love. Me mucker. Me mate. But he isn't my problem.'

Nearby, a small boy began to yell because his mum was rationing his chips.

'He's Rabin's patient,' Theo was saying, 'not mine. So we'll invent somebody. Call him Brian.'

'Brian's all wrong,' she said. 'For my chap, that is. Call him Jacko.'

Theo sighed. 'Now . . . Rabin's got you to play the game. *Guess Who I Am?* Only you need a partner, and what you get is a stinking-rich ex-Para who walks through brick walls because it's a short cut. He can't play the game, but he *can* help you, and he does. And, between you, *you* get better and even *he*'s no worse.'

Nearby, a hypermanic idiot in shorts began to do press-ups. Nipple rings, tattoos, muscles slapped on to his body like afterthoughts, and Uncle Theo didn't even notice.

'You're saying he's no better?'

'I doubt he'll ever be better,' Theo said. 'If you're there, he can just about contain it, but it's a job for life, my dear.'

No smiles, no laughter this time.

'Why not?' she said. 'It's what I'm for.'

'Voss doesn't scare you?' he asked.

'Voss?' She seemed surprised. 'Not a problem. He lost his last marble years ago. When the time comes, David will kill him and that will be that.'

The chauffeur got back in the Lincoln. Too many kids. Time to move.

I mustn't show outrage, or even censure, he thought. This is her life. Then, at last, he noticed the lumpy man and disliked him on sight.

'It's the ones behind Voss,' she said. 'The ones who wind him up and make sure his lighter's filled and turn him loose. One day, they'll die too – but finding them isn't easy. Dear God, it's not.'

She means every word, he thought, and the odds are it'll happen, and if it doesn't, she and her Para will be dead.

'Your friend Jacko and I sleep together,' she said.

'Do I need this?' he asked.

'Oh yes,' she said. 'I don't mean rumpy pumpy – though, of course, we do that too. I mean, we're both quite normal . . .' She smiled. A shy one this time. 'Oh boy, are we normal. But before. After. The same bed. Together. And sometimes he dreams and it's awful.'

'Nightmares?'

'He doesn't tell me. Even in his sleep, he sort of edits it. Crafty sod. Because he loves me. Oh, my God, he must.'

'Go on,' said Theo. The lumpy man lay on his back, pedalling furiously.

'No words,' she said. 'Not ever. Just noises. Awful, awful noises . . . So, I lie there and hold him and we make love.'

'While he sleeps?'

She nodded. 'No more pain. Just happiness.'

'Dear God,' he said. 'To think I have a niece who turned out to be wonderful.'

He scowled at the cyclist, each knee cap tattooed like a face. Laurel and Hardy. God knows where the bowler hats were . . .

'I read Rabin's notes, of course. I had to.'

She nodded. 'Of course.' 'Whip marks. Burn marks. Surgery. He should be dead. But he's like you. Obstinate. Loving . . . There'll be more dead before it's over.'

'Voss'll do me,' she said. 'He nearly ruined Ellie's life – with George's help, of course. Did his best to ruin mine. The mad major can't take care of everything.'

'What did Voss do exactly?'

'Kept an eye on me. Darling little purple pills to make sure I really was mad. Only, I let the major turn me on instead, and one day I happened to say I'd met him – David, I mean – I didn't *know* anything. I just happened to say it. To George. I mean, one had to say something to George apart from *Don't be such a bloody fool* – and Hermann the German scarpered the very next day. So did George, come to that. But not my Major.'

The Lincoln came up and cruised to a halt nearby, and acquired an instant fan club. They'll be asking for its autograph next, she thought. 'Time to get stoned, Uncle Theo,' she said. The lumpy man was doing press-ups again. His back was one vast Union Jack. Nothing wrong with that. It was where he'd anchored the flagpole . . .

There was no doubt about it. She was a big and beautiful lady. Elegant too. Evening dress. Décolletage, of course, but discreet. All the same, 'Blimey!' said Callan, then read the text below the picture. Tiffany Manners. Five foot nine inches. One hundred and twenty-five pounds. Natural blonde. Affectionate nature. Hobbies: working out, swimming, kung fu, embroidery – *Embroidery?* Carefully, he closed the book on Tiffany's photograph: a book bound in leather with a design of Cupids. Class all the way.

'She's a big girl, Rog,' he said. 'Are you sure?'

'Never more sure in my life,' said Roger, then looked about him at his living room. Luxurious, his living room. Harrods had seen to that. All the same, Roger was nervous.

'So long as . . .' His voice shook. Bad, whatever it was.

'So long as what?' Callan asked.

'She isn't an intellectoral like that Naomi.'

Calmly now. Gently, Callan told himself. This is your *mate*.

'She doesn't look like an intellectual,' he said.

'I couldn't take another one, Dave.' Roger's voice became a savage parody of Ms Klein's. '*Not serviette, my sweet. Napkin.* And, *Who wrote Gray's Elegy?* Laughed herself silly over that one . . . Then there was Newton's Third Law – I didn't even know he'd been nicked.'

'Who's been nicked?' said Callan, struggling hard.

'Charlie Newton,' said Roger. 'Used to run a pie and eel

shop down Clacton.' He shuddered. 'I couldn't take another one like that. I mean, she's nice – done a lot for me. Helped me relax even – but she's got this idea I can think.'

'That'll be the computers,' Callan said.

'But I don't think with them. I talk to them. Play games sometimes.'

Gobsmacked is not the word, Callan thought. There isn't a word known to man.

'I can't take no more, Dave. Honest,' Roger said.

'Buy her something nice,' said Callan. 'Have it delivered. I've just about got rid of her anyway.'

Roger looked at him awe-struck. Was there nothing Dave couldn't do?

'Honest?' His voice was a croak.

'Cross my heart,' Callan said, and did so. 'Who needs her? She taught me a few things early on – moving money, all that – but then she got greedy.'

'Not the stamps?' Roger had worked hard to nick those stamps.

'I told you,' Callan said. 'She's out. I wouldn't let her near. The stamps are for the big girls to play with.'

'Like your Lady Fiona?'

'Why not?' said Callan. 'They're *her* stamps. And maybe we could find one for your Tiffany, if she's a good girl and doesn't rabbit on about napkins and elegies and Charlie Newton.'

'But how would she know?' Roger asked. 'Naomi, I mean.'

Callan shrugged. 'Tell her.'

'Me?' This time, Roger's voice was a squeak.

Still gentle, Callan said, 'Roger, listen to me. I don't care where you go, who you meet, you'll be the richest man there. Money you haven't even counted yet. Girls like Tiffany notice these things. Yachts. Private planes. A little something from Cartier. It makes them happy. So, they want to make you happy too. I mean, on top of everything else – what you've got in your head this minute – you've got the lot, mate. A fine upstanding multimillionaire like you – it's your birthday, Rog. Every day.'

Roger's sigh was blissful, but even so – back to reality.

'I've got this geezer coming for a meeting,' Callan said.

'He's bringing Naomi.' And that was all it took. Roger was up and running and automatically Callan grabbed him.

'Would I do that to you? Now would I? When they come, you go and do a bit of work next door. Lady Fiona's coming. She says, would you mind taking her to the club when you've finished here?'

'Be a pleasure, Dave,' said Roger. 'Real class, your lady.'

Twelve

The hall was in Catford. A tacky run-down sort of hall, Fiona thought. And yet, it had a point to make. Rickety chairs and tables, a makeshift bar out of a Gorki play, and flowers everywhere. Dead or dying, for the most part, or artificial. And on the walls, posters fading fast: Bob Dylan, Joan Baez, Kerouac, Ginsberg, and early Beatles music: 'Lucy in the Sky With Diamonds', 'She's Leaving Home . . .' And on the floor, at the tables, middle-aged men and women in kaftans, beads, flowers. Lost youth that couldn't be recaptured: the ghosts of Haight Ashbury . . .

And beneath the kaftans, smart suits, designer jeans, expensive dresses, and an au pair and a mortgage, and perhaps an overdraft. But now, this minute, they were twenty and played a guitar and argued about Sartre. What this party needs, she thought, is some good old-fashioned fun. She went through a door marked *Ladies* . . .

An absolutely astonishing day, Theo thought. Bland, uneventful, even boring, were the days he liked – when he left the astonishment to his patients. And yet, today, he'd learned things about her, wonderful things, amazing things, and didn't mind a bit. Carefully, he looked about him. A neatly elegant man – even his kaftan had a Bond Street look. He began to panic. No sign of her – and then she called to him. 'Uncle Theo! Over here.'

He looked again. A harpy in a torn and tattered kaftan, face painted like a sunflower, chaplet of plastic daisies and a wig of unkempt, impossibly red hair, was waving to him.

A gentleman and a scholar, he went to her, like a man living a nightmare. And as he reached her, suddenly, without warning, her hair stood on end.

'Fiona, for God's sake—' he began.

'Battery,' she said. 'I got it in that shop in Charing Cross Road. Makes me look inconspicuous.'

'*Inconspicuous?*'

'I'm Lady Fiona Wilton,' she said. 'My father was an earl, my late husband a captain in the Thirty-fifth Lancers. My partner's worth millions and millions, and I do, I really do, live in a castle in Spain. Is that what I look like?'

'I see what you mean,' said Theo, and then: 'Have you spotted him?'

'Table by the exit door,' she said.

Easy, unhurried, Theo looked to where Voss and Bernardo giggled and fumbled together.

'High as kites the pair of them,' Theo said. 'You know the other chap?'

Fiona said, 'Certainly. He—'

Her uncle interrupted her. 'All I'm supposed to ask is, do you know him?'

'I know who he is,' she said. 'So does David.'

'That'll do for me,' said Theo. 'Now, you—'

'What about me?'

A mood swing like a door slammed in my face. Gently does it.

'Every bastard asks me the same thing,' she said. 'What's it like to be you?'

'Absolute nonsense,' he said. 'What I want to know is – why all this girly-girly stuff?'

'Well well well,' she said. 'You're different, all right.'

'Girlish giggles, naughty words, wide-eyed innocence. Why?'

'Explain Fiona Wilton in two hundred words. Write on one side of the paper only. But they never tell you which side, do they, Uncle?'

'Oh, get on with it,' he said.

'Why I do the mutton dressed as lamb bit? Because it never happened when it should have done. When I *was* lamb. Tender too. *Settle down*, Daddy said. Settle down! I was just nineteen and they married me off to George because they thought he was rich and Daddy needed the dosh. And George wasn't rich at all, so at least I got one laugh out of it . . . And Ellie.'

'And David?'

'He didn't give a bugger. Not from day one. Skint or rolling in it, it didn't matter. Share a bed, share a life. That's David. Because he missed out on the early years too. All he got was the orphanage, the Paras, the nick. Only, he can't act it out for himself.'

She breathed in then. Not a sigh, he thought. Only love.

'And that's enough about your giggling, wide-eyed niece,' she said. 'Now it's your turn.'

'What you've just told me – I'll never tell. You know that. But I honour you for it. And the pair of you, loveless children. Even now, after half a lifetime. Of course, you invented parents. Only, sometimes he's your father, sometimes you're his mother. Nothing more likely.'

'Spot on, Uncle Theo,' she said. 'No wonder you're the King of the Loonies.'

Theo said tetchily, 'How many times—' but already she was looking past him.

'Phoebe,' she called. 'Darling. How marvellous.'

Hunter and attendant lords. One seemed relaxed enough, but the other was Pancho. Pompous Pancho. He carried a tray with water and glasses and was far from happy. Was he in pain, too? Hunter motioned to the water jug. 'Well water,' she said. 'Organic, I'm told. A freebie, and no wonder. It's ghastly.'

'Good thing I brought my lift-off pill,' Fiona said, and produced a vast and threatening purple substance. 'Cover me, darling.'

Hunter sat very close to her. 'Honestly, this wasn't my idea,' she said.

Fiona crunched her pill. 'Fatso?' she said. 'It smells like him.'

'Now, just a minute,' Pancho said.

Fiona swallowed the pill and took a sip of well water, and at once her hair stood rigidly on end, then slowly subsided as Pancho looked at the people nearby, none of whom took the slightest notice, then glowered at the two women.

'Don't you ever do that again,' he said. 'That's an order.'

Fiona looked at him, thought Theo, as she might look at a

gun dog that simply wasn't up to it, and turned to Charlie. 'Have you thought about a choke chain?' she asked.

'Just let him say his piece,' Hunter said. 'Get it over with.'

Fiona clasped her hands and stared adoringly at Pancho.

'As a result of recent enquiries,' Pancho said, 'I have reason to believe—'

'He's not real,' said Fiona. 'He can't be.'

'You go on like this and you'll be nicked,' Pancho said.

This time the hair rose slowly, like a curtain, and Fiona cried and sobbed – louder, louder – then winked at Theo as Hunter hugged and comforted.

'There, there, Feefers,' she said. 'The nasty man didn't mean it.'

'He bloody did.'

Hunter considered, then said, 'Well . . . Yes. But it's only because he's thick.'

She tried to move away, but Fiona clung to her.

'Oh, please don't leave me, darling!' Then: 'Oh my God, I can see two of him . . . It's dreadful.'

She sat up, hands making the namaskar, and began to chant, 'Om . . . Om . . . Padom.' And still no one reacted. Just one more chant. 'Om . . . Om.' And Hunter chanted too. 'Great Krishna help her,' as Fiona boomed 'Padommm!' and a flower child sprinkled them with rose petals.

'Go for it, sweetheart,' he called. '*Om*, man. *Om*.' But then, he really was tripping.

Fiona stopped at last. Her hair twitched, then was still, and Pancho turned to Theo.

'What the hell's she on?' he asked. Theo shrugged.

'She's on something,' said Pancho.

'We can do her for possession.'

'No,' said Theo. 'Rabin and I both sanctioned it.'

'Rabin?'

For the first time in years, Theo lost his temper. 'For God's sake,' he said. 'You blundering oaf. Don't you know anything?'

Beside him, his niece talked on a mobile. 'Whiter Shade of Pale' was playing. Far more relevant than the Beatles somehow.

'Yes . . .' she said. 'Yes, of course.' Then, in her best Battle of Britain voice, 'Wilco, sir . . . Jolly good show . . . Over and out.' She turned to Theo.

'Giggle time's over. Back to HQ, I'm afraid.'

'First you tell us which one your son-in-law is,' Pancho said, and his brow furrowed. 'I don't understand what he's doing here anyway.'

'He's here to kill me,' Fiona said.

'Why doesn't he, then?'

'First he has to smoke a joint and grope a member of the male sex. He's doing it now.'

'And then he'll kill you?'

'He'll try,' she said.

'Ha bloody ha,' said Pancho, and Fiona sighed. Uncle Theo was right as usual. *Oaf* was the only possible word.

'A lot of officers sweated blood on this one,' he said. 'Do you think I'd waste their time on a hash-happy queen?'

Fiona turned to Hunter. 'He's out of his tree,' she said. 'Shall I tell him?'

Hunter nodded.

'The table by the bar,' she told Pancho. 'Don't look round till Hunter tells you. Hash and a grope. Just as I said. I blame the kaftans. Such a temptation.'

A group of Hare Krishna monks approached them, robes of saffron, cymbals clinking. Voss was looking over for Fiona, but they obscured his view, and when the monks moved on, Fiona and Theo had vanished. Only a box of Smarties marked where they'd been.

In the street outside the building where, in Fiona's words, peace and love were so madly popular, Melissa, William and Mars sat in the rear of a Merc 600 with CD plates and a flag on the bonnet, playing brag. Melissa and Mars wore business clothes, William tribal robes. Suddenly Fiona and Theo appeared and headed for a Bentley – Roger wouldn't expose his Lincoln to flower power – then Fiona turned, waved to them, and lifted her hair by way of farewell.

'God, she's gorgeous,' said Melissa. The Bentley whispered away and she yawned. 'But she's gone. Time to be bored again. Tell you what. Come back to my place and I'll cook you a missionary.'

William yawned in his turn.

'You're no gentleman,' she said.

'Oh yes I am,' said William, as Mars talked softly into his mobile.

Mars stressed the words: 'On her way.'

'It's just that at home we never eat missionary after five o'clock,' said William. 'Gabby women . . . Yes.'

Melissa, at her sweetest, said, 'You know what? Fiona was wrong. You don't look ridiculous in a skirt. You'd better watch that.'

There was a tap at the window, and Mars pushed the button. A policeman, blast him. He must ask Melissa if they tasted as good as missionary.

'Playing cards,' the copper said. 'You know that's illegal.'

'Playing snap's illegal?' said Mars.

'You weren't playing snap, sir.'

'I never said we were,' Mars said. His mobile buzzed and he answered at once: 'Embassy limo.'

The policeman sighed, and made his way to a Ford Fiesta that looked far from well.

'I told Roger,' Mars said. 'She's on her way . . . She's fine. Voss? Still in the den of iniquity . . . Yes. Hunter too. Do you want us to— Just as you say, David. Whatever turns you on. Ciao!'

He turned to the others. 'The Mighty One has spoken. Voss has to catch that plane no matter what.'

'And Bernardo?' Melissa asked.

'I rather think the gay caballero's become surplus to requirements.'

'But that's no reason to look so bothered,' she said.

'Not that. No,' Mars said. 'I asked him about Pancho and he said he'd handle that himself.'

'Oh dear, oh dear,' said Melissa fondly.

When she arrived, they appeared to be having some sort of meeting. The Mighty One, Roger, Pancho and his chum, Hunter. She'd been home to change – they were going dancing, after all – and to get rid of the sunflower. Beyond taking off his kaftan, Pancho seemed much the same and Hunter looked elegant. She always did. Get on with it, she thought. He can't eat you, though she could think of worse ways to go.

'Darling,' she said. 'Not late, am I?'

'Well, of course you are,' said Callan.

'That's all right, then. The trouble is, Uncle Theo had to visit Dr Rabin. His affliction, you know. So painful, poor man. Uncle Theo says they're as big as—'

'Let's save it for our memoirs,' said Callan. 'You remember Roger?'

'Yes, of course,' she said, and offered her hand.

'Delighted, My Lady.' His voice was hoarse.

'And these three?' said Callan.

'Not three. One plus two,' said Hunter firmly.

'Hooray for you, darling,' said Fiona, and kissed her cheek, sat down beside her.

'Haven't we met before?' Pancho asked.

'She was—' his mate began, but Pancho had come to talk, not listen.

'Belt up,' he said. 'I'll handle this one.'

His mate sighed. Fiona thought he must do a lot of sighing.

'Voss? No trouble there?' Callan asked.

'Well, he didn't kill me,' Fiona said. 'Too busy having fun. But he didn't know me, any more than Bernardo did. Far too busy you-know-whatting.'

'And the wig?'

'Sensation,' Fiona said. 'Wasn't it, Feebs?'

'I haven't laughed so much since they launched the Titanic,' Hunter said.

'And really crocked?' said Callan.

'Wings of a dove,' said Hunter. 'Two doves, I mean . . . Good smack, delicious gropes . . .'

'That's the kaftans,' said Fiona. 'Sort of emergency entrance, if you follow me.' She looked at the fast-track wonder. 'Why, Pancho,' she said. 'You've gone all blotchy.'

'By God, you were there!' Pancho said. 'Seven men I had on that job. Twenty-eight hours' overtime. And you— you—'

'What did *I* do?' Fiona seemed bewildered.

'Sweet nothing, that's what you did,' Pancho said. 'That's what you all did. All I needed was two words: *That's him*, and we could have lifted him. He might have led us to Bishop.'

Callan looked at Hunter and the shrug she gave said as clearly as words: *Yes I know. But what can we do?*

'But no,' Pancho continued. 'All you could do was rabbit on to that uncle of yours.'

'Nonsense,' said Fiona. 'I did pick him out. To my friend here.' She nodded at Hunter. 'I picked out Bernardo too.'

'But not to me,' Pancho said. 'I was in charge.'

Hunter looked at Callan. It was his turn to shrug.

Fiona, not bothering to lower her voice, said to Hunter, 'He does it on purpose. He must do. Nobody's that much of a—'

'And another thing,' said Pancho. 'This job's stuffed with bloody amateurs. I mean, what's he doing here?' He turned on Roger, discreetly elegant in an Ermenegildo Zegna dinner jacket.

'Bugger off,' he said.

Roger looked at Callan. 'Roger stays,' Callan said.

'Oh, does he?' said Pancho.

'Unless you want to work the computer yourself.'

'Alright, he stays,' said Pancho, thwarted but still punching. 'But he does what I tell him.'

'And gets us all killed?'

There was a collective sigh, as if they were in a cinema and the hero was strapping on his guns – Hunter apprehensive, Fiona ablaze with excitement. Only Roger was relaxed.

'Don't interrupt me,' said Pancho. 'This is important.'

Callan turned to Roger. 'Did he speak?' he asked.

'Now, Dave,' Roger said. 'Remember what the doctor said.' They were deep into a well-rehearsed routine. Serious, as actors are serious, but loving it.

'Just ignore it, you mean?' said Callan. 'Pretend it never happened?'

'Nice to be nice, Dave,' said Roger.

'Will you two stupid berks belt up?' Pancho was yelling now.

'He *did* speak,' said Callan.

142

Pancho stormed over to where Callan sat. 'You bet I—' he began, and Callan hit him. It was a vicious and accurate blow, delivered by an expert, an expert's expert, and Pancho dropped like a brick in a pond.

Callan got up from his chair, kicked Pancho out of the way, and went to his mate. 'You want some of that?' he asked him. Fiona, still at the cinema, said, 'Oh, super,' but Pancho's mate stayed where he was.

'No, no,' he said. 'I'm fine, thank you, guv.' He looked at Pancho. 'Never better.'

Callan clapped him on the shoulder as Roger said reverently: 'A copper called Dave *guv*. What a night.'

Callan rubbed his fist and Roger took a bottle of champagne from the ice bucket, and passed the bucket to Callan.

'Thanks, old son,' said Callan, and let the ice soothe his knuckles.

I bet I'm spinning like a Catherine wheel, Fiona thought, and there he stands. So . . . so *grey*. Like a stone.

She dropped a cushion on Pancho and sat, and Pancho groaned. 'He's terribly out of condition,' she said, and prodded his stomach. Another groan. Then she looked brightly, crazily, at Roger, because Roger too was a film fan, and this was his big scene. Carefully, Roger grasped the bottle, popped the cork, and turned to his guests.

'Champers anyone?' he said.

Still in the limo, still parked outside the peace and love hall, Melissa and William played war-to-the-death battleships. Mars kept well away, and Melissa yelled in triumph as she won, crossed out the figure seven on the paper, and wrote eight.

'You cheated again,' said William.

'I did not,' she said.

'Oh yes you did.'

'Oh no I didn't.'

'Did did did,' said William.

'Didn't didn't didn't,' said Melissa. 'So there.'

'Knock it off,' said Mars. 'The opposition's arrived.'

They looked to where a Scandinavian car, PC to the last

hubcap, was squeezing into a parking space. Naomi, Avram and even the chauffeur, all in kaftans, headed for the hall.

Melissa donned a wreath of battered flowers and looked in the mirror.

'Daisies,' she said. 'I might have known.'

Thirteen

In Roger's flat, he and Fiona chatted to the sound of Glen Miller's Pennsylvania 6-5000 and Callan took a phone call. 'No . . . You hang on in there. Tonight we start to earn. Keep calling . . . Pancho? He had one of his turns . . . Hold on, I'll ask.'

He turned to where Roger was talking to Fiona, saying, 'Sunningdale. Some right hoarders. Makes it a lot easier when they hoard.'

'Hey, mush!' Callan called.

Fiona turned to him, but Roger winced. That was no way to speak to a lady.

'Did one of your devoted slaves get rid of Pancho?' Callan asked. The band was loud, but Roger loved it like that. She went to Callan.

'A perfectly sweet SAS man got rid of him,' he said to the phone. 'No no. He's as secure as you are. He better be. He's Roger's minder.'

He hung up, then dialled again. 'Let me speak to Wendy,' he said. 'This is Tinkerbell.' He snarled into the phone. 'You heard.'

Fiona said, 'I wish Gerald wouldn't do that. It upsets David dreadfully – and you know what he's like when he's upset.'

'So does Pancho,' Roger said.

'Yes . . . Well . . . Never mind that. David says you want to talk about your new girl.'

'I need your advice, My Lady. Only, first – Dave and me – we got a feeling we should settle something.'

'Settle what? Nicking hoards down Sunningdale?'

'This is serious,' he said, and she begged pardon.

145

'You got a few bob, My Lady,' he said, and at once the mood switch came, like a light turned on.

'If that bastard's trying to give me money . . .'

But they were talking about theft, and Roger was a master. 'Nobody's trying to give you money,' he said. 'All you'll get from BC Electronics is your director's fee, and believe me, you'll work for that.'

'I'm sorry,' she said. 'Forgive me. Please. But the thing is, I don't *have* any money. We used to – not by your standards, but quite a whack by most people's. Only, it sort of disappeared.'

'Well, Dave and me's reappeared it, so to speak,' said Roger.

'So now I can go to Bond Street on my own?'

'Any time, My Lady. You see, Dave and me did a job a while back—'

'My old nanny could explain it. She could explain anything. *Satan finds work for idle hands to do.* Big job, was it? The White House? The Elysée Palace? The Vatican?'

'Grosvenor Place,' said Roger.

'Not exactly Fort Knox, but no doubt you needed the practice.'

'A geezer called Voss lives there sometimes,' Roger said. 'He—'

She interrupted him. This could be tricky. 'Tell me honestly, Roger,' she said. 'Am I going to like this?'

'You'll love it, My Lady,' Roger said. 'Just let me tell it.'

'Once upon a time,' she said. 'Too bad I forgot my teddy.'

'First we took . . . some stuff . . . that told lies about a very special person indeed. Our pride and joy, you might say. Then we took back your stamps. Reclaimed them, David says.'

'Roger, I never collected stamps in my life,' she said.

'Voss did. Collected yours, come to that. What I mean – he paid for them with your money. Easy, really. First he conned your husband into selling up – converting into cash—'

'But how could he?' she said. 'The bank would have told me.'

'More than one bank in this wicked world. And some of them's naughty. Andorra, Liechtenstein, would it be? Even Russia.'

Suddenly she sat up straight. The angry, crazy look returned. 'You mean it,' she said. 'You bloody mean it.'

'Of course I bloody mean it,' said Roger, then put his hand to his mouth. 'Beg pardon, My Lady.'

'Over six hundred acres,' she said. 'A hundred and seventy-three Aberdeen Angus, a manor house, a farm, machinery, equipment and a couple of hunters – and he swapped it for a book of stamps?'

'Not a book,' Roger said. 'These.' He handed her a photograph of the stamps.

She looked at them, taking her time. They were hers, after all. Pictures of ancient aircraft, and men with leather helmets, goggles, the occasional white scarf; tough yet somehow touching young men. Nine of them. Nine bloody stamps for all she once had worked for, pulled back from the edge of disaster.

'Ah well,' she said. 'I suppose they're worth something.'

'Oh yes, My Lady,' he said, and then: 'If I may ask, how much was your home worth?'

'Ask away,' she said. 'It wasn't a home – not after Ellie left. Just a sodding great millstone with a marvellous view.'

The music changed. Fats Waller, 'Ain't Misbehavin'. Goodness, David must be feeling old. Still telephoning. Now he was scribbling notes, too. And all for Voss?

'Seven fifty, maybe eight hundred K,' she said. 'And the stamps?'

'If you don't mind, My Lady,' He reached for a house phone, pressed one number.

'Philippa?' he said. 'Of course it's me, you old queen. Who did you expect? Arnold Schwarzenegger? Of course it's the stamps. Last offer, you stupid berk. Don't you *gay rights* me. Check out that Greek geezer. The one with the ships and the airline and the telly stations . . . That all? Find me another one quick. Her Ladyship doesn't like to be kept waiting.'

He hung up and turned to Fiona, who had watched, round-eyed. 'Poofs is murder,' he said.

'Except when they're doing one's hair,' she said. 'How much?'

'One point three million,' Roger said, and Fiona screamed as she'd screamed when she'd found she owned an Alfa.

147

'Torture,' said Callan into the phone. 'Yes, I *know* it's agony, but nothing else works. We just cancelled her aromatherapy.'

Fiona said, 'Roger. Darling Roger. Please be patient with me. I'm not as young as I was. *Would* you mind saying it again. Rather gently.'

'One point three million,' Roger said. This time the scream diminished to a squeak.

'Money,' Callan told the mobile. 'I only ever torture for money. Not like this Kraut I met once.'

Fiona turned to Roger. For once, she seemed bewildered.

'Why didn't *he* 'tell me?' she asked.

'He did tell *me*,' said Roger, 'so I could tell you. At least, he thought he did. But mostly it was all Zippos and the Hilton from hell. In the end he says, "Tell her. You're a mate. You can do it." Then he says, "Nothing for George's lot. Not a tosser," he says. "It's all hers . . . Money she earned, bless her." ' Roger finished there, till at last he said, 'OK?'

'Absolutely super,' she said. She looked at Callan, still talking.

'Spain,' he was saying. 'The hacienda . . . Because that's the way I've set it up . . . No, you can't be a nun. Not in Spain anyway . . . And Torremolinos to you, amigo.' He hung up.

'Hey, mush!' Fiona called. 'Thank you for my prezzy. I've always wanted one of them.'

'One of what?' he asked.

'A million . . . There is just one tiny thing.'

'How did eight hundred K become one point three million?' he said.

'That's the tiny thing. Half a million quid.'

'Oh, that,' he said.

'Yes, that,' she said. 'And, whatever it is – don't try it.'

'But it's so simple,' he said. 'Like, when we nicked them they were worth eight hundred K. Right? Only the price went up.'

'Half a *million*?'

'Half a million.'

She looked for something to throw, settled on a tumbler of heavy crystal, and Roger said, 'If you don't mind, My Lady. That's antique Waterford.' He passed her another glass.

'Just listen,' Callan said. 'You can start throwing when I've done. You can afford to, after all.'

She put the tumbler down.

'Look at them,' he said. They're all early American airmails, right?'

She nodded.

'Only, after we nicked them, they became more popular. Don't ask me why. Collectors are even barmier than we are. Anyway, they went up three hundred K for starters. They'll make one point two easy.'

'It's the truth,' said Roger. 'Honest. Philippa's checking it out now. You could ask him, if you don't believe me.'

'No, I couldn't,' she said. 'But there's still a hundred thousand gone adrift – I mean, I realize it's just loose change to you two . . .'

'You sure you want to know?' he asked.

'You know what I'm like. I *have* to know.'

Callan turned to Roger. 'We used the computer. Better you tell her.'

Roger said, 'We didn't use Philippa . . . Rosie . . . She's a bit slow, but she's got a lovely nature – and thorough with it.'

Again Fiona got the dazed look, she who'd always, always known what she would do, but Roger was in another world that she could never hope to reach.

'There was a hundred grand in fivers,' said Callan. 'Used, unused, clean, dirty. A few had blood on them. We reckoned it was heroin money.'

'And pretty nasty at that price,' said Roger. 'Cut with anything you can think of. But they all queued up to chuck their lives away. Twenty thousand of them – poor sods.'

'And you've given it to me?'

'Not given, My lady,' Roger said. 'It's yours.'

'You want me to give it away? Drugs charities?'

'If it's what you want,' Callan said.

'Of course it is. A hundred thousand pounds and I spend every penny. Me . . . Fiona Wilton. Giving giving giving!'

'Are you going to tell Dr Rabin?' Callan asked.

'He'll love it,' she said. 'Oh, God bless you both.'

149

She looked round for Roger, who was talking on the mobile.

'Rosie, my love,' he said. 'Nice to hear your voice. You sound great – no, honestly.' He covered the mouthpiece and turned to the others. 'A real sweetheart, is Rosie,' he said. 'Only, it doesn't pay to rush her.' He returned to the mobile and Fiona and Callan stared like children at a magician.

'Who told you that?' he asked. 'Philippa? I might have known. Put him on, would you? Ta, love.' To Fiona he said, 'Philippa reckons that the Greek will go another fifty. Top whack. That do you?'

'I'll leave it to you,' Fiona said. 'You're the expert,' and Roger became a giant as they watched.

'Philippa?' he said. 'Now, just you listen to me. Fifty's rubbish. Get me a hundred. Quick. How? How should I know? That's what I made you for. To suss out money. If I'd wanted truffles, I'd have made a pig . . .'

They looked at him, awed, as he hung up. Callan cleared his throat. 'Why—' But his voice squeaked and he tried again. 'Why don't you two go to the club now? Celebrate? I'll be along as soon as I've done my bit of business.'

She looked at him. A hundred grand for junkies didn't come cheap, it seemed. 'Promise?' she said.

It was his turn to look. *Oh my God*, the look said, *What did I do to earn this happiness*? 'Promise,' he said, and passed the catalogue to Roger.

'Show her your dirty pictures,' he said. 'And don't start worrying about Naomi. Fiona'll protect you. And, anyway, she's coming here.'

Roger left at once, Fiona followed and Callan turned down the dimmer switch.

In the peace and love street, Mars and William fretted and waited. No peace at all, thought Mars, and not much love either, till the grass, the pills, the coke began to bite. And then she appeared at last, not even hurrying. Yuk kaftan, Woolworth's beads, plastic daisies and all, she looked like the Queen of Hollywood . . . The two men left the car, went to her.

'We were coming to look for you,' William said.

The worrier, she thought. There's always one, and it isn't Mars. Relaxed as an alcoholic in a brewery, Mr Mars.

'I'm OK,' she said. 'Those Mossad spooks were playing hunt the Voss. No sign of him.'

'There wouldn't be,' Mars said. 'David rang. He reckons Voss left Grosvenor Place ten minutes ago. Plus chum.'

Melissa moved behind the car and the two men followed to watch Avram and his team leave the hall. None of them looked happy.

'We still hang on here?' Melissa asked.

'We get Voss on that plane no matter what,' William said.

Melissa sighed. 'We *do* live, don't we?' she said.

El Alamein was reaching its climax. Rommel was running out of inspiration, fuel too. The British artillery was blasting at the Panzers like fairground ducks in a barrel, and the hard men were moving in for the kill. Fifty Div, and fifty-one. 'Blaydon Races', 'Scotland the Brave'. Nearly dark now, but the flash of the guns was like lightning. Only thing was, it was all black and white. But the booms and bangs were terrific.

Callan moved back into the pool of darkness he'd constructed so carefully.

'Will you stop this nonsense,' Avram said. In the light, silly bugger.

'In a minute.'

Grey men on grey sand. Lee Enfield 303s. Dear God, it could have been Wellington at Salamanca. And then the bagpipes and the whistles and the seeming chaos that wasn't chaos at all, but men moving off to kill. Close-up of a young subaltern doing his best to look like Vlad the Impaler. On the screen, he could have been twelve years old. *Here it comes*!

A shell screamed louder than all the others, then seemed to explode in Roger's drawing room. Virtual reality. Roger's little joke. Callan watched delighted as Avram dived for cover, Naomi Thing screamed even louder than the shell. Roger *would* be pleased.

'Will you please turn that thing off?' Avram said.

'No,' said Callan, 'but I'll compromise.' He turned the sound down. 'More than you're doing, old son.'

'It will do,' said Avram. 'Be quick. I have things to do. *Important* things. What do you want?' He looked at the screen. 'You and your stupid toys.'

'You're bloody rude,' said Callan. 'I'll say that for you.'

'What do you want, *please*?' Avram said. 'Will that do?'

Callan looked again at the screen. The ripped cloth noise of a Schmeisser firing a burst, the whip-crack sound of the thirteen-pounder that blew it to hell. You could see the bodies fly like acrobats – except they didn't get up. Telescopic lens, that would be.

'I want Mossad to stop trying to steal from me,' he said.

'Now you're being ridiculous,' said Naomi Klein.

Behind him, a machine gun chattered. A British machine gun. All the back-up he needed to chat up a lady.

'Klein, you're not concentrating,' he said. 'We're talking big money here. Enormous money. Mossad would do a lot for big money these days. That's why they needed a plan. That's why, with one voice, they cried, *Send for Naomi Klein*, and you duly obliged. And not a bad plan, either.'

The bagpipes squealed and Callan winced.

'General Sherman was right,' he said. 'War *is* hell. But you didn't know, did you? Not then. Not when you planned to have me killed, me and my ball and chain and my mate. Because we weren't real people to you.'

'Then what were you?' she asked.

'Chess pieces. A knight, a queen, a king. Mate in three. Not human at all, and that made it painless. And that made it easier. I understand.'

Avram said, 'Don't listen to this nonsense.'

She spoke as if she hadn't heard him. 'It's a good plan,' she said. 'But it wasn't mine.' She looked at Avram. 'And it isn't quite complete.'

'A piece missing?' said Callan. 'A bishop, maybe?'

Avram said again, 'Don't hear him. I forbid it.'

'Of course you do,' said Callan. 'You screwed up. Two million. Sure. No more than a win on the lottery, if that.

So, take it and bugger off, Dave, and don't bother to write. So, I went and killed a couple of blokes and there it was. Two million times twenty-five. Fifty million quid's worth. Diamonds, mostly. Hundred dollar bills for pocket money, and all for me, and Avram's the biggest berk in Israel.' He glanced at the telly. A long line of prisoners. Hundreds, maybe thousands: the invincible Afrika Korps. 'The man who gave away fifty million. That's some trick.'

'You're the one who does tricks,' said Avram.

'Sure,' said Callan, 'I did some for you, remember?' and Avram said nothing at all. Now *there* was a victory. Change target. He turned to the woman. Naomi Klein MA, barrister-at-law. 'Now, Klein, old top,' he said. 'To win the coconut, why should anybody give me fifty million quid?'

'But it's ridiculous,' she said. 'You're saying we just let you keep it? *Fifty million?*'

Back to Avram.

'Would you like to tell her?' he asked, but Avram looked at Hitler instead. Like Avram, Hitler wasn't happy. He'd have to do it himself.

'I was an embarrassment, love. Mean to say. Fifty million. If I sold it to the press, they'd make it fifty-one. Callan had to go. Otherwise, he'd make Mossad look silly. Best way was to give me back to the East Germans. They'd be happy to oblige. And there I'd be – romping with my chum Voss all over again. Only, there was no East Germany to—'

'Mossad wouldn't do that,' she said. 'After what you did for our country. Give you back to that sadist . . .'

'"No details," they said. That's what the top men always say. They're busy men. They've got a country to protect. So, they sent for Avram and told him to get on with it.'

'Avram? But you saved him . . .'

'That was a detail,' said Callan. 'Like the floggings, splinters under the nails, fire. Not like Joan of Arc. A bit at a time. Their money's worth, so to speak. Avram thought he was home and dry. Bloody fool.'

'Why a fool?'

'They'd lifted him once. They could do it again. And it

153

would all be down to Avram. Mossad would be whiter than white, as the saying is. Let's hope he looks under the bed at night.'

'But you escaped them?'

'For now,' said Callan. 'It's like this, sweetheart. This time round, all I wanted was money. But the first time – what I did for Israel was a debt they couldn't pay. But this time, it was only money, and for all they knew I was telling the truth. So, somebody came to see me – a very high-up somebody – and tipped me off about my old friend Avram, and I killed three geezers. Two ex-Stasi. One KGB.'

The madness flickered like sheet lightning.

'They're part of the M4 these days.' He looked at his watch. 'Busy time for traffic. Not that they'll be bothered.'

'But I thought that happened in Spain,' she said.

'That was another lot. Avram likes to keep me busy. Smethy an' all.'

That one hurt, but she kept going. Good girl.

'This will be your life?' she asked. 'On and on?'

'No,' he said. 'Voss has run out of foot soldiers. Next time, it'll be a DIY job for both of us.'

The telly showed a picture of a bulldog smoking a cigar and waving a union jack, and a voice said, 'El Alamein was a Chatterbox production.'

'You live and learn,' said Callan. 'I always thought it was Montgomery.'

The screen went blank and Callan waited, and so did Avram. Time to get him started. Bad show to keep a lady waiting – especially his lady.

'That first time,' he said. 'When the Wall came down. Tell her about my face – if you're man enough.'

And, because he needed her, Avram told her. He had no choice. But all Klein could think of was zeros. Seven of them, and a five in front.

Callan pressed a button on the zapper, and she saw a naked man, bearded, skinny, his face – oh, dear God. Two male nurses supported him.

'That's me on my hols,' Callan said. 'Months and months in the Negev. Away from it all. I'm the one in the middle.'

154

Casually almost, he continued, 'Dear old Avvers was next. He's the chap who wants to rob me.'

'But . . . you didn't talk,' she said. 'How could you not?'

'Voss would have gone on regardless. *There*'s a chap who really enjoys his work. Loves it, even. And I'm far too bloody obstinate, anyway. All the same – soon I would have cracked, only, the Wall came down, and your boss will never know the thrill of a lighter flame next to the skin. Unless I do it – eh, old friend?'

And still Avram didn't move. Ah, well. If at first you don't succeed.

He turned to Klein.

'But Israel took care of me. The best they had. First the physicians, then the surgeons, then the fitness guys. They put me together like a jigsaw puzzle. Only, when I was fit again – the walking miracle, they called me – I was a bloody nuisance.'

'*Nuisance?*' she said.

'Well, of course. Mossad had some top-secret stuff in the Negev holiday camp. But they couldn't just shoot me. What would the CIA think? Mossad's the good guys.'

'So, they set up this lottery for me. One prize. KGB treasure. All the dosh I could carry. And either way, they won. If I missed, the Ivans would shoot me, and if I hit – it was KGB money anyway. Fine. Everybody happy. Only, like I say, their computer got its sums wrong. Avram too. And that's about it – eh, Herr Obersturmbannführer?'

Avram winced. 'I am so bad?' he said. 'Listen to me. Please. What you did for me – every day I thank God for what you did. Every day. But Israel is even more important. Fifty million. Is that twenty pounds for every man, woman and child in Israel – or all for Callan? Take the finder's fee. We give it gladly. But Israel must have the rest.'

Callan turned to Naomi. 'He does it well, doesn't he?' he said. 'I bet he's a smash at Hadassah. I had a little weep myself.'

Something wrong with Klein. Wriggling in her seat, and not from well-bred Inns of Court lust.

'Something wrong, love?' he asked.

155

'Please,' she said. 'The picture. Can't you change it?'

He pressed the zapper at once. Avram had got the message anyway. They were now looking at bronzed, fit, beautiful young men battling it out in a game of basketball. And he was one of them, as bronzed and beautiful as the rest.

'Better than beagles, eh Klein?' he said, then to Avram: 'Trouble is, you've been screwing up just recently. Right, old friend? Not the golden boy any more – and a brass boy who needs, as the monkey said.'

She was looking at him, the woman they'd sent him. Too soft, too clever, and always questions, thought Avram. He was losing her. One year on a kibbutz and he'd asked for a sabra.

'It's for Israel,' he said. 'I swear it.'

Again Callan's gaze flicked to the woman.

'What is it they say in *Vogue*, sweetheart?' he said. 'About something marvellous?'

Her voice a whisper, she said, 'It's to die for.'

'*Vogue*,' Avram said. 'Gossip. Dresses. Perfume. We are talking about Israel. Our country.'

She stood up to face him.

'We've talked enough about Israel,' she said. 'Callan is bored and I don't blame him. Tell him you're sorry and leave him to it.'

He hit her one-handed, and she fell hard. He could still hit, Callan thought, and risked another look at her. Not spark out, but dazed. She really did have very nice legs. Cellulite not a problem.

'Get up,' Avram said.

Bloody fool. Now was the time for *please*.

Somehow, she got back into her chair, picked up her handbag.

The basketball players glistened with sweat. Still, not so poofy as baby oil. Callan moved in the shadows, and thought, Far too close together. Bloody fools.

'You'll like this bit,' he said. 'Look.' Some fast, intricate play and then a basket.

'That was me,' Callan said. Klein touched her face. The bruise was already a delicate plum colour. Poor love.

He pressed the zapper again. A blast of gunfire, but it was

Avram who jumped. In the desert, the beautiful young men were firing at targets, and an instructor watched, praising sometimes, blaming often, the way they do, and the film cut to Callan, shooting on his own. The instructor watched and the zoom lens showed the target, wild-eyed and sinister as Rasputin, until the bullets slammed home in neat, precise lines. Then he reloaded. Heckler and Koch .308. Telescopic.

'Ms Klein makes sense,' Callan said. 'Go away, Avram. Scarper. On your bike.'

'Without Israel, I go nowhere,' Avram said. Ms Klein snorted. Not nice, but sincere.

'Forget Israel,' said Callan. 'Money's what it's all about, and this morning Ms Klein had lots of money . . . Dollars . . . Thousands and thousands of dollars.' He shook his head at the wonder of it. 'From Mossad? I don't think so. Say the word *Israel* and Avram reaches for his begging bowl – eh, old friend? How about *international* dollars . . . Washington, then Moscow, then Andalucia? Makes sense – eh, Avram? Andalucia?'

'That is Israel's money,' Avram said.

'Do me a favour,' said Callan. 'Isn't that what you say? It was Smethwick's money. He'd jump me, kill my nephew, and sell me for cash. No discount. No wonder Ms Klein was upset.'

'Prove it,' said Avram. 'Go on, then . . . It's nonsense.'

'A German for a friend,' said Callan. 'Oh, Avram – how could you? A little chat in Spain. Another in London . . . Peace and love, eh Avram? But it's OK. All that happens is I'm a little bit richer, so how about a deal? Tell me where Bishop is, and I'll give you a million.'

'How should I know where bishops are?' Avram said. 'I'm a Jew.'

Ah well. It had been worth a try.

No reaction this time, thought Callan. Any minute now. Then it's Plan B and drinks all round. Klein runs Roger, and you run Klein and Israel loves you and Mossad adores you. Happy days are here again. The small arms rattled once more, and at last Avram looked at Klein and made his move, produced an Israeli piece Callan hadn't seen before. But the

157

magnum seemed to jump into his hand and he shot Avram in the shoulder. His gun dropped and Callan shot him again in the kneecap and he fell. They were even. 'I told you I was mad,' he said. 'Why didn't you listen?' Klein listened, still as stone.

'God this place is dreary,' he said, and touched the zapper button, and that was mad too, because now they were in a beach café, people in beach clothes, a Jewish fiddler playing 'Raisins and Almonds' and, in a corner, Callan arm-wrestling a basketball player, and winning. Somehow, she knew that when he lost, whatever the game, he would die.

'That's better,' he said. 'Can I get you something?'

For a heart-stopping moment, she thought he might call a waiter from the café – supposing the waiter *came*? – but he reached out for glasses, a bottle of Piper Heidsieck. As he did so, Avram groaned. 'Don't start that,' Callan said. 'We've heard quite enough from you. Now, mind, I mean it.'

He could have been talking to a class of eight-year-olds, but even so, Avram stopped groaning.

He went to Klein, looked into her handbag at the little Bernadelli .32, held in place by a spring clip.

'He screwed up, didn't he?'

'I'm sorry?' she said, and because the bewilderment was genuine, he explained.

'The old one-two,' he said. 'You distract me by going for your gun and he shoots me. Only, you didn't. Why not?'

She just sat there like an idiot. I can't even answer him, she thought.

'Shall I tell you?'

She nodded.

'He'd just hit you. His only friend, and he walloped you. Hard. And his idea didn't make sense anyway.'

She swallowed and said at last, 'Well, it didn't. If he'd killed you—'

'Not killed,' he said. 'Immobilized. He wanted to kidnap me.'

'For Israel?'

'For Roger.'

'But that's crazy . . .' She looked at him appalled, but all he did was smile.

'Tell me why?'

'Because you'll never give him up. Half the SAS are round him like a wall. Avram couldn't match that. Ever.'

'Like you say, he's crazy. Believe me, I know. Israel *needs* Roger. So, Israel must have him. Avram too. The Golden Boy again. So, off to the lion's den he goes.'

'Mossad would never sanction that,' she said.

'Of course not. Avram's trying a little private enterprise. But us capitalists – we tend to hang on to what we've got . . . Take him back. He needs a spell in the Negev holiday camp.'

'But – forgive me – will I—'

'You'll be all right, love. Innocent bystander . . . Cross my heart.' Suddenly the madness struck again.

'Did I ever tell you about the time I killed this young geezer in Shepherd's Bush underpass?' he said chattily.

In the limo, Melissa catnapped. William and Mars played snap, and Mars lost.

'Sod that copper anyway,' he said.

William looked in the car mirror. 'Never mind the copper,' William said. 'We're on.' Up the street, Voss and Bernardo got out of a minicab. Bernardo staggering, Voss holding him up. Ecstasy? Mars wondered. Certainly not hash. It didn't have the punch. They somehow reached the hall, then the alley behind it, as William shook Melissa awake and Mars left the car, and William, still in his robe, went into the hall.

Melissa linked arms with Mars and they strolled easy, relaxed, to the top of the alley, watched as Voss reached a spot close to a half-open fire door, then produced a hypodermic and injected Bernardo. The Spaniard's legs kicked out in spasm, then he was still, as Voss poured the contents of a gin bottle over him. A torn peace and love poster lay nearby, and Voss put it on Bernardo's face, added the last of the gin, then fumbled in his pocket and produced the Zippo lighter. Mars moved then, but Melissa grabbed his arm.

'He's dead, baby,' she said.

Carefully, Voss set fire to the poster, then went to the door marked *Fire Exit* as the flames took hold, the poster peeled away.

'Dear God,' said Mars.

'Big bucks, baby,' said Melissa. 'The biggest.'

Voss looked back, checked his work, then went in through the door.

In the peace and love hall, Voss smoked a joint and William watched from the edge of a multi-ethnic group – white, brown, black – until Melissa and Mars appeared. The music played. 'Golden Brown'.

'Where's Bernardo?' William asked.

'Passed away. It was all very peaceful,' Mars said.

'Not where he's going,' said Melissa.

Two policemen came in wearing kaftans. They looked like Cinderella's ugly sisters. Voss saw them at once, put away his cigarettes and Zippo, and went to the bar for a small well water. The ugly sisters were working their way to the Gents.

'David won't like this,' said Mars. 'Voss'll leg it when they get close.'

'Can't have that,' said Melissa. 'You follow them and be unkind. I'll keep an eye on Voss for now.'

'Give me the stuff,' William said, and she handed him a plastic bag, and the two men left her as a group of kaftans went to the bar, all guitars and tambourines, and began to sing, ignoring the piped music. 'California Dreaming', was it? Who cared. It blocked Voss's view and made Melissa smile . . .

Carefully, obsessively even, a policeman washed his hands. This place would be crawling . . .

Behind him a polite upper-class voice said, 'Excuse me,' and the policeman turned. Facing him was a nightmare apparition: a fiend from hell, tattooed face, fangs dripping blood, its hair a screaming, impossible red. As he watched, the hair began to rise, slowly, inexorably, from the horizontal to the vertical.

The detective wanted to scream, but found that he couldn't and fainted instead. William caught him deftly and Mars emerged from a lavatory cubicle to make room for the policeman, and they suspended him from a hook on the door. He too looked peaceful, Mars thought.

There was a sound outside and William stood behind the main door. Mars turned, fiddling with a tap as the second copper came in. He started to look round and William hit him.

Mars spun like a dancer and fielded him. William took off his wig, and they hung up the second copper next to his chum.

'Don't forget your teeth,' said Mars, and they went back to the hall. No Voss . . . No Melissa, but they didn't worry. Melissa was gorgeous, but she was also tough.

Callan said, 'And that was about it. One dead. Two for the hospital, by the look of them.' He thought for a moment and said, 'One of them was crying.'

'You didn't call an ambulance?'

'I doubt they'd call one for me,' he said. 'Anyway, it wasn't one of Avram's better jobs.'

'*Avram*?'

'He had to make space for you,' Callan said. 'Only, it didn't work, so he hired some local talent.' He looked at Avram. 'Eh, Herr Obersturmbannführer?'

Avram groaned. He couldn't help it. He wanted to tell Callan so before he kicked him again, but he couldn't speak.

'He's bleeding an awful lot,' she said.

'Not a *lot*,' said Callan earnestly, once more the teacher with the promising student. 'Magnum bullets are really quite neat. But he's made a mess of that sofa. *And* the carpet. Roger hates shopping for furniture – but I expect you know that. Harrods?'

She nodded.

'I'd better do it. Tell Mossad I'll send them the bill. Stupid bastard. He's useless with a gun. You want him out?'

'Please,' she said, and then, because she couldn't help it, 'It's not just greed, you know. He means well.'

'It could be his epitaph,' said Callan, and picked him up. More blood. More bills for Mossad. She led, and he followed, and Avram groaned. He's strong, but he doesn't look strong, she thought, no bulging biceps. Just . . . fit. For anything he decided to do. At the door, he stayed in shadow and she went to the street, waved to their car. The chauffeur came up at once and she opened the car door, and Callan threw in Avram like a sack of potatoes, then went back to the shadow of the house, looked at her and said, 'Shalom.'

Naomi Klein felt as if she'd passed some sort of exam.

161

Fourteen

S he was where they'd expected her to be, on the edge of the action. A fire engine was parked down the street, but the crowd was gathered by the hall door, where policemen tried to persuade them to go home, without success. Mars shed his kaftan and he and William went to where Melissa was talking to the most senior policeman she could find, a fat and flustered man who resented women telling him that the road must be cleared *at once*, especially black women, pretty ones with jewellery his wife could only dream of. He turned to the black giant in a skirt with a damn sight more respect. William was making a phone call in some language he'd never even heard of, but hung up at last. 'His Excellency,' he said. 'We must go now.' In Spanish he added, 'Voss came out and took a minicab. Airport.' Then Melissa started yacking in Cajun. She knows perfectly well I don't speak Cajun, William thought, and replied in Classical Greek. Hazily, Mars realized he was quoting Aeschylus, *The Persians*, and wished he had a camera, especially when Melissa burst into tears.

'Sad news indeed,' William said. 'Terrible. We *must* go back to the Embassy.'

The policeman looked at the crowd. 'I'm afraid that's impossible,' he said. Melissa began to yell. 'Racism. Prejudice. At such a time. H.E. will see your Prime Minister . . . Your Queen. She is good, your Queen. Not a racist pig in a uniform.'

The crowd began to applaud and the policeman thought, *That's all I need*. Well-heeled hippies with a cousin in the House of Lords.

Then Melissa burst into tears again, the crowd looked nastier than ever, William patted her shoulder and switched to Virgil. Suddenly Melissa turned to Mars, clung to him, her body shaking. The crowd sighed. Only Mars knew that it was laughter she hid. Then she broke away, stood straight and tall, defying the policeman to do his worst, then turned to Mars. 'You too,' she said. 'You too, Murgatroyd. You also are a kaffir. Because you help us. White kaffir. For you too the sjambok—'

'The whip,' said William.

'The terrible whips of the oppressors. But they shall not hurt you. With my own body I protect you. I swear it.'

The crowd cheered, and the policeman came up warily. He was almost smiling.

'We've cleared a path,' he said. 'Want me to guide you out?'

'Of course not,' said Mars, and put on his chauffeur's cap.

Merc 600. It *would* be, the copper thought, flag and CD plates all in order, but he'd do that bloody chauffeur. Dangerous driving at least. Then he found he was watching a master. The big car seemed to dance down the road, past the fire engine happily squirting, and in the back William gravely bowed, Melissa blew kisses, and not once did he brake or check his speed. For him, an inch of space became a foot.

Once clear of the hall he took his cap off, cracked on a bit till he picked up Voss's car, then eased off. They could pick him up any time they wanted.

'So, when are you going to protect me with your own body?' he asked.

'Just as soon as Ellie says it's OK,' said Melissa.

He's smiling, she thought. Something happened a while ago, but now he's smiling. We can all relax. She looked up at Roger, coping rather well with 'Blue Moon', but still Callan smiled. Even when the mobile rang.

'Fire?' he said. 'Any casualties? No. Leave the body count to the rozzers. You just see our chum into the departure lounge. Pancho's mate takes over from there . . . You three watch the take-off. I'll see you in the VIP lounge.'

He hung up, and signalled for more champagne as Fiona and Roger joined him.

'You never told me what a super dancer Roger is,' Fiona said.

'Right little Fred Astaire,' said Callan, and waited as the wine arrived.

She touched his hand. 'Tell us – if you can,' she said.

'Bernardo's gone to meet his Maker,' said Callan. 'Bit of a shock for both of them.'

'David!' said Roger. 'That's blasphemy.'

'I don't think He'll mind,' said Callan. 'He gets enough of the miseries . . . Anyway, Bernie had a bit of help.'

'Voss?' Fiona asked.

Callan nodded, and Roger stirred in his chair. Not uneasy. Terrified.

'If you want to skip this hand, old son . . .' Callan said, and Roger, bless him, was indignant.

'I can't,' he said. 'You're my mate.'

Callan smiled. 'Then he started a fire,' he said.

'Didn't he like the well water?' Fiona asked. 'Not that I blame him. It was foul.'

'Spot of confusion. Too many coppers and he had a plane to catch.'

The band played 'Smoke Gets in Your Eyes', and Fiona said, 'Come on, Twinkletoes. Your turn.'

They danced in the forties style, like the others. It was why they'd joined in, after all.

He danced well but, 'You've been working hard tonight,' she said.

'Who told you?'

'Nobody. But you're twanging like a fiddle string. Are you all right?'

'I thought we all were,' he said. 'But there's something I've missed. I know there is.'

Her hand covered his mouth. 'Not now,' she said, and moved in closer. 'Roger's big day tomorrow. I've been sort of advising him. OK?'

'Fine,' said Callan. 'He gets the counselling. I've got the counsellor.'

'Oh, *you*,' she said, and then: 'I told him to wear an Armani suit. Has he got one?'

'Last I heard, he had seven,' said Callan. 'Where will they eat?'

'Belle Amie,' she said. 'Then Bond Street.'

'Not a hope,' Callan said. 'Belle Amie'll be booked till next year.'

'I rang myself. The full Lady Fiona. Consort of the joint chairman. Director in her own right.'

'Let's hear it.' Callan sounded wary.

'They somehow got the idea Roger might be going to buy the place. You know – don't over-chill the champagne cocktails, and make sure the caviar's beluga. Mr Bullevant is *very* fussy about his caviar. So, that's it. He and his guest will be there tomorrow. Table overlooking the park. OK. Yah?' She smiled, and looked up at him.

'OK, yah it is. Let's go home,' said Callan.

Back to their table and Roger was worrying about which suit to wear. There simply wasn't time to buy another one.

'Leave that to me,' Fiona said. 'Let's talk about posh names.'

'It's the computers,' Roger explained. 'They need a bit of class. Well, I mean – Rosie's a bit common, and that Philippa – I've had the silly old queen up to here.'

'How about Emma and Cressida?'

Roger was ecstatic. 'I might have known,' he said. 'Real top drawer . . . Perfect.'

'That reminds me,' Callan said. 'Show the nice lady your dirty pictures.'

Nearby, a waiter was listening hard as Roger produced the leather-bound menu from his briefcase and Fiona turned the pages. The waiter made his appearance to top up their drinks, took one look and left them to it.

'They're not dirty, My Lady,' Roger said. 'Honest.'

'Of course not.' She patted his hand. 'They're gorgeous. Which is Tiffany?'

Roger showed her.

'Oh, I say,' she said, and this one wasn't part of her act. This one she meant, thought Callan.

'She's a big girl,' Fiona said.

'I like them big,' Roger said, and Callan smiled at him fondly. Say what you like about my mate, he thought, but at least he was reliable. Whatever the place, whatever the occasion, Roger would always say the wrong thing.

He finished his drink. 'Time we were off,' he said. 'Early flight. You could do with an early night as well.' He looked at Tiffany's photograph. 'Busy day for you tomorrow.'

'Gawd, I hope so,' Roger said.

Callan thought: Definitely the time to go. 'Just promise me one thing,' he said.

'Well, of course,' said Roger.

Callan looked once more at Tiffany's portrait.

'Be gentle with her,' he said.

From the VIP car park, they watched the plane's lights glow in the night sky.

'There she goes,' said Mars. 'Dead on time.'

'Right. Let's go and see the boss,' Melissa said, and turned to William.

'Put your pants on, lover.'

William found a case and began to change, as Melissa said, 'You know, I'll really miss that dress. It turns me on like crazy . . . Why, William Wilberforce Fitzmaurice. Don't tell me you're blushing?'

'How the hell would I know?' said William.

In Andalucia when they woke, the sun was already warm. Fiona, in her bathrobe, yawned and stretched, then lay back down on the trampoline bed as Callan came in, damp from the shower, and lay beside her.

'We missed the nightingales,' she said.

'Gala concert tonight,' he said. 'They don't do matinees.'

'They remind me of you,' she said. 'All drab and nondescript—'

'Thanks very much,' he said.

'Then suddenly they do the most amazing things.'

'I wouldn't mind doing an amazing thing right now,' he said.

'Not yet,' she said. Today's a working day, remember.'

He was about to speak when there came the bang and clatter of builders' materials from outside. Scaffolding, planks, awnings, tools.

'I never knew a garden party could be so noisy,' she said. 'Only, it's not a garden party, is it? It's cheese.'

'Cheese?'

'For the rat-trap.'

'Voss?' Callan said. 'He'll do for now. My blokes need the practice. Bit of fun, I suppose.' And maybe a bit more than that, he thought. But where's the sense in giving My Lady the screaming abdabs? I've got enough for two.

She sat up on the bed. 'Is that all he is?' she asked. 'Fun?'

'He's a bit more than that when he reaches for his Zippo.'

He stretched out, relaxed. 'Gerald got word from London. Forensic. Bernardo. Voss had given him a right going over before he killed him. About time he moved on. He was having too much fun.'

As he finished, Fiona jumped to her feet, her fists clenched, and she yelled out loud. '*Oh, sod it, sod it, SOD IT!*'

Callan sat up. Easy, relaxed, or so it seemed. 'You're wishing it had never happened—'

'Well, of course, I—'

He interrupted her. He almost never interrupted her. '—That we'd never met. That you were still broke. That Voss was rogering George twice nightly and Saturday matinées.'

'You have such an elegant way of putting it,' she said, and then: 'You're saying we can't win.'

'No more we can. None of us. Voss, Bishop, Avram, you, me. The good guys *and* the bad guys.'

'Hard to tell them apart, you mean?'

'Sometimes. But there is a way. The bad guys don't care.'

'About what?' she said.

'About anything,' he said. 'Whatever it is, they don't care. Like how Voss gets his jollies. It may not be their idea of fun, but if it works, don't knock it. My love, these men aren't *nice*, and that's why I've got the job.'

'You?' Fiona said. 'A *job*?'

'To stop them,' he said. 'For the love of Fiona. Ellie. Roger, come to that.'

167

She went to the dressing table, began on her hair, her make-up, and he massaged her neck, coaxing away the tension.

'You keep this up and we'll have to go back to bed,' she said.

'Yours to command,' he said.

'Only we haven't time. We never do have bloody time.' She looked at him in the mirror. 'So, how do you get *your* jollies?'

'You can sit there and ask me that?' he said.

'I just love to hear you say it. Why me?'

There was an envelope on the dressing table. He picked it up.

'Where would I find another one like you? You're beautiful, elegant, foul-mouthed—'

'It was you who taught me the words,' she said.

'Let me finish . . . Brave too. And the best right hook at your weight I ever saw. Of course I love you.'

He opened the envelope, took out the contents. 'When did this come?' he asked.

'When you were swimming. Embassy messenger,' she said. 'Sorry. We got sort of involved.'

Callan shrugged, and took out copies of a photograph. Naomi, Avram, Callan, the chauffeur, grouped round the Israeli car, the colour of their faces an impossible yellow. Night-time in Mayfair.

Fiona looked at them all, then back to Avram. 'Is he drunk?' she asked.

'I told you,' he said.

'Oh,' Fiona said. Now it was different. Now she could see it. 'So, Ms Klein's the bad guy,' she said at last.

'Sometimes. Sometimes it's Avram.' He thought for a moment. 'He loves too much.'

'Don't we?'

'We love what's possible. What's real. But him. It isn't a woman . . .'

'Like George?'

'It's not a man, either. A cause. An ideal. He can't love people. He's tried.'

'Trying's no good,' Fiona said. 'You just do it.'

He put an arm round her, turned over Avram's happy snap. Four words. It was all he needed. 'Not the regular chauffeur.'

In the hacienda grounds, workmen were putting up the garden-party stalls: a hammer and bell to test your strength, airguns, darts, a coconut shy, a tiny slide and an equally tiny roundabout for tiny people. Ice cream, cola, lemonade. A four-year-old's vision of paradise.

And, dominating the display, drawn up in line, Wellington's finest: riflemen in green, line infantry in red, facing a furious charge of French cuirassiers, all cut out of hardboard. Mars and William in T-shirts and jeans acted as advisers, which involved sitting down a lot, but then, yesterday had been a trying day.

'David's late,' said Mars.

'Don't rush him,' said William. 'We can cope.'

'You old softy,' said Mars, and went to the front rank of riflemen, drew an imaginary sword, and pointed dramatically at the French cavalry.

'At least I get my chance to command men,' he said.

They had moved into the dressing room, and Callan too wore T-shirt and jeans, and worked on the Suvorov cannon yet again. Fiona wore a flowing gown of fine translucent silk that distracted him in a most satisfactory manner.

'What are you going to do?' she asked. 'Hit him with it?'

'Kill him with it,' Callan said, still working on the cannon.

'Darling,' she said. 'I'm all for what you're going to do – honestly I am – but, please, no details, Mighty One.'

He twisted the gun barrel and the gun limber, spring-loaded, flipped open, became a box.

'No details,' he said.

She sat on his lap and squirmed, her hands caressed him.

'Fiona, for God's sake,' he said.

'Tell me you don't like it and I'll stop.'

'Of course I like it. I adore it,' he said.

She giggled. 'Let's romp, then,' she said.

'When I've tidied the War Room.'

She looked at him. 'Voss?' she said, and he nodded.

From the garden, William's voice boomed. 'A Company!'
Then Mars's voice. 'B company!'

Fiona wriggled again, and Callan picked her up, then set her down on her feet.

She looked at him. 'Well, at least we know it still works,' she said, and walked towards the balcony in a flutter of rose pink and sapphire, but he caught her by the waist – not hurting her, she doubted if he could ever hurt her – and held her back in the shade.

'Those are impressionable lads out there,' he said. 'They've got work to do.'

'Why, you're jealous,' she said.

'Well, of course I'm jealous.'

From below, the whip crack of Mars's voice. 'Front rank. Aim. Fire!' Then William's voice echoed his, and the cuirassiers tumbled as the rifles and muskets cracked.

'Dear God,' she said. 'Even lumps of hardboard. So real. How old do you have to be to play this jolly game?'

'Twelve and over,' he said.

'*Twelve?*'

'Same age as Wellington's drummer boys.'

'It's always death with you.' But her voice was gentle.

'It's all I know.'

'Oh no it isn't,' she said, and turned in his arms, the pink and blue turned to gold.

'Let's romp. We can't just stand here thinking up ways to put out Voss.'

'Not *put* out,' he said. 'He's not a drunk in a pub. *Take* him out. That's what we say. *Take* out Voss.' He picked her up again.

'I even bought a new hat,' she said.

'Later, love,' he said. 'We can't just waste it on a quickie.' He carried her back to the bedroom; put her down.

'You know, what I love about you is your romantic nature,' she said. 'Venice by moonlight. Fluttering candles, and violins sighing away like billy-oh; turtle doves that—' Her voice became a gasp and then: 'Oh, have it your way,' she said. 'Let's do the music-hall routine.'

*　　*　　*

170

Outside was the rhythmic sound of the French meeting Wellington, and not doing terribly well. Second rank. Aim. Fire! Third rank. Aim. Fire . . . !

William moved through the black-powder smoke to confer with Mars.

'Jolly fun, what?' said Mars.

'Dear God, how could they do it?' said William. 'Woollen uniform, boots like a diver's, weapons a professional strong-man couldn't handle . . .'

'Iron men, in those days,' Mars said. 'But it seems a lot of trouble to kill just one man – even Voss.'

'Every usable gun in the place has been locked away,' said William. 'The guardia came and checked. The antiques on display don't work, and Voss knows it.'

'And the garden party?'

'Helps him to get in,' said William. 'Cover.'

'Let's hope The Mighty One's in form,' Mars said.

'How can he miss? He's got Wellington on his side.' William looked up at Callan's balcony, then at his watch.

'Leave it,' said Mars. 'Tell me the drill again.'

Fifteen

In the gardens, Mars toiled away at turning a children's roundabout. William sat on a tiny pony. 'And that's it,' he said. 'Happy ever after.'

'Seems OK,' said Mars. 'Whose idea was the piledriver?'

'One guess.'

'Fair enough,' said Mars. 'Voss is lucky, in a way. He won't even know. All the same, it's time to go. Don't worry. He'll be fine.'

'Does that go for Fiona too?' said William.

In their dressing room, Callan and Fiona did their double act in bathrobes, straw hats and greasepaint moustaches. 'I say, I say, I say,' said Fiona the star. 'My dog doesn't eat meat.'

'Why not?' said Callan, the stooge.

'I never give him any. Mind you, I come from a posh family . . .'

'Geroff,' said Callan.

'It's true. They were in the iron and steel business.'

'What's that then?'

'My mother used to iron and my father used to steal.'

Callan switched on a tape recorder. The laughter was tremendous. It faded and Callan said, 'And now, to send you on your way with a smile, a little song entitled—'

Fiona twirled, curtseyed and said, 'Get off the Gas Stove, Grandma, You're too Old to Ride the Range,' and, to the thunderous applause of the tape, the band played 'Me and My Shadow' as Mars's voice called from outside, 'Second Rank. Aim. Fire!' A volley crashed out, and Callan and Fiona danced to the music. At last, Callan went to the dressing table and began to remove his make-up as Fiona danced on.

'Fiona,' he called, but still she danced, unheeding, and he called out again. 'Fiona.'

'I'm *dancing*,' she said, but he spoke to her anyway.

'You're getting better,' he said. 'Rabin's cut down the pills to one a day. Right?'

Fiona slammed down the stop button, stormed over to Callan. 'You've been having me watched, you bastard,' she said. 'Who was it? William?'

'John,' Callan said. 'William's tomorrow.'

'I'll kill that bloody John. He's supposed to like me.'

'He loves you,' Callan said, and she looked at him incredulously.

'Wha-a-t?' she said.

'Not like I do. That's Ellie's department. More like an aunt. The most gorgeous, glamorous aunt—'

'And that's why he spies on me, I suppose?' Fiona said savagely.

'That's why.' He was utterly serious. Slowly, the rage died as Callan continued. 'It's why he risks his life for you too. Voss is a fool, but he knows his stuff. You better hope John does too. And William. If they don't, they're dead. Not just a little bit dead. Dead all over.'

'I – I love them too. Like you said. I don't want them to die for me.'

'You think there's a choice? There's only two kinds of minders, believe me, like it says in the prayer book – the quick and the dead.'

'Couldn't we just go away?' Her voice was pleading, but he shook his head. 'Why not?'

'You're valuable, love,' Callan said. 'Unbelievably valuable. If the bad guys get you, they get me – and Roger. And if they get him, they get all he's done: all he will do. We're not spies any more, we're capitalists, like every crook I ever met. They don't want *Das Kapital* or *Mein Kampf*. They want a billion dollars. And we're the ones who've got it. They want *us*. Ladies first.'

'There must be somewhere,' she said.

'Well, of course. Beautiful places. Only, we'd have company.'

173

'Company?'

'Maybe a CIA team rehearsing for World War III. Or an SAS team who used to wrestle polar bears till the animal rights mob objected.'

She went to him. 'Hold me, please,' she said. 'Just hold me.' And when he did so: 'I didn't *know*. How could I? But I knew I loved them.'

Outside their door William cried out in a high-camp voice: 'Ten minutes, please. Stand by, actors. Ten minutes, please.'

Callan said, 'Sweetheart. Listen to me. Please. I know I said we were all losers. But not today. Today we win.'

The look she gave him went on and on, as if his whole life was written in his eyes, until at last, troubled yet loving, she smiled, and began to remove her music-hall make-up. She stepped into a blue and white Empire dress that could have been Josephine's favourite, as Callan checked his rifleman's uniform.

'Will John wear that?' she asked. 'And William?'

'Not William,' Callan said. 'He's in scarlet.'

'My God,' Fiona said. 'He'll look like an old-fashioned phone box.'

'And lovely with it,' said Callan. 'It was his idea. He's used to scarlet anyway. He was in the Irish Guards.'

'Oh, come *on*,' Fiona said.

'He *was*. Honest. He loved it. Best fast bowler they ever had. Best prop forward, come to that.'

'But didn't they play him up?'

'*William*?' said Callan. 'You've got to be joking. They were terrified of him. And if one *was* naughty, William would give him extra unarmed combat and he'd be the enemy.'

She'd been smiling, delighted for her friends, then suddenly she slammed down her hairbrush.

What's the charge this time? he wondered, and said at last, 'You want to hit me now or talk first?'

'Why should I want to hit you?' she asked.

'You look upset.'

Suddenly her voice was a yell. 'I'm not upset, I'm flaming bloody mad! All right, clever clogs. John followed me. Fine. No problem – but he wouldn't know Dr Rabin said I was—'

'Improving,' Callan said. 'No. Somebody else did that.'

'Uncle Theo,' she said. 'My own bloody family. Even the nice ones . . . Of course I'm going to hit you.'

'At least put your glove on—'

But it was too late. She hit him in the stomach and then yelled aloud, and tenderly rubbed her fist.

'Why don't you listen? Just once?' Callan said, and took a sponge and a bottle of arnica from the drawer and dabbed her knuckles.

'Don't you ever fight fair?' she said.

'You knew it would happen,' he told her. 'It always does.'

'Bugger that,' she said. 'You're no gentleman.'

'Well, of course I'm not,' he said.

'He admits it,' she said, and her eyes looked up to heaven. 'You hear that, God? He admits it.'

Outside, William, still camp as a Boy Scouts' outing, was calling, 'Everybody on stage for the Hawaiian number.'

'Well, of course,' he said. 'If I was a gent, I'd be with a lady . . .'

She grabbed for a bottle of cologne, but he was too quick for her, held her wrist.

'But I'm not with a lady. No way,' said Callan. 'I'm with a goddess.'

She looked at him warily, then. 'Oh, *you*,' she said.

'All the same . . .' he said.

'*Now what?*'

'If I was you, I'd finish your shave before we make our big entrance.'

Fiona looked in the mirror. A bit of the music-hall moustache was still there. The Charlie Chaplin bit.

Sixteen

The air was warm, but there was masses of shade, and awnings and ladies lightly clad, and ice cream and a Genghis Khan horde of children, all in costume: flowered dresses, poke bonnets, befrilled shirts, midshipmen's jackets. By the rose garden, in place of nightingales, a bewigged octet played J.C. Bach, Haydn, Mozart – and Fiona twirled a parasol and contemplated flogging a midshipman,

'No,' said Callan, before she had even moved.

She sighed, but he was right, sod him. She was the hostess, and the guests were watching avidly. All that wealth. All that expensive splendour, and yet their hostess's father was the seventh earl. Sneer or cringe? And suppose they got it wrong? And their friends: a black giant who was once in the Guards, a rifleman who couldn't wait to shoot somebody, Angel – *the* Angel – like a caballero by Goya. Their hostess's daughter in a dress like her mother's, except that Ellie's was much more white than blue. A gypsy dressed like a princess. And then the black – lady. It was the only word. Melissa. Elegant and yet sexy, as if, just once, *Vogue* had joined up with *Playboy*. And in *pink*, of all colours. But such a pink. The orchid among the roses.

'This,' said Fiona, 'is what money is for.'

Callan eased his rifleman's stock. 'It's what our money's for,' he said. They looked at it: gleaming, colourful, *rich*. More early Goya.

'The best setting money can buy,' he said.

'Setting?'

'For a jewel,' he said. 'My jewel.'

'If I start to blush, I'll kill you,' she said. When he looked at her, she was close to tears. Change key, Callan.

'You remember that time you hit me with a horseshoe,' he said.

'I never did,' she said. 'You wriggled out of the way as usual.'

'I'd bought you some earrings, only you said you couldn't be bought.'

'Well, I can't', she said.

'I wasn't trying,' he said. 'It was a bribe.'

'You told me that too, because you said it was fun being bribed . . .'

'I remember.'

'And you went straight out and bought me an Alfa Romeo. For God's sake – when are you going to stop?' she asked.

'Maybe never,' he said.

She snorted, and somehow contrived to nod graciously as the mob closed in and Mars, easy, relaxed, drew Callan aside.

'I saw him,' he said. 'In the car park. Like a priest, the way they were two centuries ago. He looked like an old oil painting.'

'More like a tombstone,' said Callan, and Mars looked at him. No laughter. Not so much as a chuckle.

'Same drill?' Mars asked.

'Do me a recap.'

'I try to keep him out of the War Room, but he talks his way in, so I hit the buzzer—'

'And go to work. William too. Go for it, John. Oh . . . Take your watch off first.'

He never misses a thing, thought Mars. It was a Rolex, for God's sake. Elegant. Discreet. But Wellington's army didn't even know what a wristwatch was.

And so Voss got as far as the gardens, looking at soldiers, roundabouts, hoopla, darts, stopping by the test-your-strength machine. A large man brought down the hammer with tremendous force, the bell rang and the audience applauded. The large man handed the hammer to William, and Carmencita squeezed his arm. Mars, watching, thought: For the honour of the regiment. The world's most unlikely Irishman. The

177

hammer crashed down, the bell rang, and Carmencita leaped into his arms, twisted and squirmed and blew kisses left and right, but not to the clergy.

Voss strolled on, and Fiona watched him, her fan held close to her face. He knew her, of course he did, but he must not see the hate. A man dressed as a Velasquez nobleman came up and hid her anyway, but he was jolly hard to get rid of.

Voss reached the door to the hacienda, and at once Mars appeared. Behind him, on the first, gentle hills, he could see the bonfire. Waiting. Ready. A good omen.

Mars said, 'Sorry, Father, the house is closed to visitors.'

Voss held up a printed sheet of paper. 'But in your programme it says, *The War Room may be visited.*'

'Short-handed, I'm afraid,' said Mars.

Voss began to sweat. He *had* to get inside. Callan was there. He'd seen him go. No gun. No bodyguard. His best, maybe his only chance.

'But it is the period of history I study,' he said. 'I'm writing a book. Could I not take just one look? Please?'

Mars looked hesitant, unsure. Voss thought, I'm going to win. 'I am a priest,' he said. 'Just let me look. I will touch nothing. I swear it.'

Slowly, reluctantly, Mars said, 'Five minutes, Father, no more.'

'God bless you, my son,' said Voss, and in he went.

Mars took a small piece of plastic from his pocket, pressed its one button, said softly: 'Will you walk into my parlour,' and turned to where William was standing by the soldier cut-outs and talking with two twelve-year-old generals, impatient for war. Mars took off his hat, mopped his forehead, and at once William came to him, not quite running.

In the War Room, Callan heard the buzzer and sighed his relief, then went back to work. The farmhouse, Hougoumont, that Wellington had used as a kind of fort, and caused more casualties than anywhere else, even at Waterloo. Carefully, he adjusted the roof of the farm, then examined the Suvorov cannon, put it down and poured a glass of brandy, watched his hand shake. Might as well do the alcohol bit as well, he thought. It's a once in a lifetime show, after all. Then the voice he would never forget said what it always said before the romping began: 'Guten tag.'

Slowly, reluctantly, Callan looked up and there he was, old-fashioned soutane, shovel hat; only the 9mm Makarov was out of place.

'Oh my God,' he said, and Father Voss loved it.

'You fool,' he said, overacting as always. 'Did you really think we'd let you go? Both hands on the table. Schnell!'

No harm in that. It brought his hand closer to the model farm. He put down the glass, but made his hand shake first so the brandy spilled, then waited as Voss took a Zippo lighter from his pocket and lit it.

'No, no. *Please*,' said Callan, and his whole body shook. Voss's last treat.

'Quiet, my son,' he said. 'Your penance will come later. You have my stamps here?'

Callan nodded.

'Get them.'

Callan pushed the gun and limber to him, and Voss balanced the lighter, still burning, on the table, then slowly moved it to where Callan sat.

'You want to burn?' he said. 'Even before you are dead?'

'No, no. Wait,' Callan said. 'The stamps are in the gun limber. Pull back the barrel. See . . .'

His hand reached out, but Voss snatched the gun away, like a child holding on to another child's toy, then pulled back the gun barrel. 'And now?' he said.

'Turn it,' Callan said. 'To the right.' When Voss did so, the limber became a box, the lid sprang open, and William's voice bawled at them from the garden. 'Front rank. Fire!' and a volley crashed.

Callan doubted if Voss even heard it. He was looking at the stamps, tipping them from the limber on to the table, the Makarov nice and handy. Suddenly he yelled in rage and looked again at the stamps. They were the kind children collect: Popeye, Olive Oil, Bluto.

Callan tipped over the farmhouse, grabbed for the gun

inside, a double-barrelled pistol, 1800, say. Fired a ball the size of a marble, as a small boy's voice squeaked, 'Second Rank. Fire!' Too late, Father Voss. Far too late. The pistol boomed in time with the rifles and muskets outside, and Father Voss departed this life. In his mind, Callan quoted Fiona. It really was the most tremendous fun. Even so, he waited. No harm in making sure. 'Third Rank. Fire!' William bawled, and Callan fired too, the impact of the bullet knocking Voss out of his chair.

Callan took a pull-through and cotton rags from a drawer as Mars came running, while outside, William exchanged salutes with the two twelve-year-old generals.

In the War Room, Mars clapped Callan on the shoulder and took the pistol, continued to clean it. Callan walked to the main door, where William loitered on the steps, ready to move, and the place glowed with happiness, thought Callan.

'Come and join us, Major,' William said. 'Sure, you're very welcome.' His Irish accent was impeccable. Callan strolled on and looked to where Fiona, Melissa, Carmencita and Ellie gossiped furiously; and then the music began again, but this time it was for a dance of the Spanish court – stately, elegant. Fiona looked away and saw him, and smiled, ecstatic, then curtseyed to him, and he bowed in return.

'Time to dance, ladies,' Fiona said, and they danced. The crowd came flocking, and Callan watched, then strolled back to the War Room, where William and Mars worked at frantic speed, easing Voss's body into a huge sack already stuffed with inflammable junk. Callan picked up the pistol from the table and returned it to its place in the stand of arms mounted on the wall, then helped the others to load the body on to a scruffy garden wheelbarrow. As they lifted the sack, the Zippo fell out and Callan picked it up, looked at it, then dropped it back in. William and Mars had shed their tunics. Beneath were T-shirts. Mars listened as the octet struck a chord and different music played.

'You're on, Nureyev,' Mars said. 'Your public awaits you. Go out there and knock 'em dead. Oops. Sorry.'

*   *   *

In the garden, the women danced, then Callan appeared, and one by one they left the floor till only Fiona remained. Carmencita said softly, '*Olé, guapa,*' as Callan appeared and gravely, elegantly, they danced.

Seventeen

In a beaten-up old pick-up truck, William and Mars approached an area of scrub land covered with wrecks, cars,
vans, a camper, even a bus. Nearby, a piledriver waited
as they passed a notice: *Compañía BC – Destrucciónes Per
Acuerdo*. Mars chuckled. 'Nice one,' he said. 'Destructions by
Appointment.' He looked again at the piledriver – brooding,
ready – then drove the pick-up closer to it . . .

In the hacienda garden, the two of them danced, and two
hundred years rolled back like film. Softly, Fiona said, 'OK?'

Equally softly, Callan said, 'Never better.' In the far, far
distance a bell rang . . .

They'd tossed for first go, and William had won. One more
ring of the bell and he pressed the button, the hammer slammed
down, and Mars took pictures.

'What is this?' William asked. 'Next year's Christmas
card?'

'Didn't I tell you?' said Mars. 'The Mighty One asked
me . . . Like he really wanted to be sure.'

'Can you blame him?' said William.

Mars handed him the camera and rang the bell once more, as
Fiona and Callan danced, and Callan tried to look at his watch
and remembered he hadn't got one, but the chopper would be
OK. Of course it would. Roger and him – they owned it. And
even if Angel wasn't the pilot – not this time – they owned
him too. One of the good guys.

Mars loved it. It would take them away. The two of them
– and the messy parcel that once was Voss . . . And then it
came. William, sprawled on the grass, looked at it as if it was
nasty beyond belief.

'God, how I hate those bastards,' he said.

The music had stopped, the ladies chattered and Fiona thought, We've done it. We must have done. The FO *will* be pleased. And them – elegant sods. All Lords and Twickers and Ascot. And use us crazies to do their killing and sleep like babies . . . And still no sight, no sound, no way to check the time. Then Angel came to them and bowed. If I live to be ninety, thought Callan, I still won't be able to bow like that, and then – as the ladies curtseyed in reply – and then the chopper sound, chugging like a Toy-Town train. It flew over the gardens and the guitarist struck a chord, the dancers took their places and began. Two men, the crowd saw, two lucky ones, a soldier in bottle green, menacing but graceful, and then at last a black giant in scarlet. The dance was complete.

The crowd had gone at last, and the two of them could shower, relax in dressing gowns, and, for Fiona, a mantilla too, that slipped when she moved.

'What does *olé, guapa* mean?' she asked.

'Who said it?'

'Carmencita.'

'Sort of, *Go for it, sexy*,' said Callan.

'And I did, didn't I?' Fiona said. 'It's funny . . .'

'Laugh a minute,' said Callan.

'A bit odd, though,' she said. 'I mean, you killed him and then we danced and you-know-whatted and I feel marvellous . . . Don't you?'

'He was a rat,' Callan said. 'I'm glad I was the terrier.'

'Was it quick?' she asked.

'Bang bang.'

'Far too good for him.'

'You want it slow – call the Gestapo,' he said.

'Don't think I wouldn't . . . You like my hat?'

'The best yet,' Callan said.

'Only, it isn't a hat. And *not* for an Indian Goddess.'

'It *is* for my Indian Goddess.'

Like a reflex, she said, 'Oh, *you*,' and then: 'Uncle Theo.'

'Nice man,' said Callan. 'But not now . . . If we can't play goddesses and peasants, let's eat. I'm starving.'

'Afterwards,' she said. 'Food's always afterwards.'

183

'Are you going to hit me again?' he asked.

'This is serious.'

'So's chorizo.' He sighed. 'Let's have it.'

'He asked me about you – something personal – and I said I didn't know, but I can guess.'

'Go on.'

'All that torture. That ghastly pain. For two days. You almost died. Suffered hellfire – but you didn't talk. For a man you didn't know. A man who's trying to cheat you. For God's sake, why didn't you *tell*?'

'I couldn't,' said Callan. 'For a day and a half, he just burned me. No questions. Just jolly fun. Five minutes on – then two hours off to get me ready for the next one.'

'But why? I mean even Voss—'

'To soften me up. To make me think there was only pain. For ever – and he enjoyed it, anyway. And afterwards – when I was good and ready – the Wall fell down. Humpty Callan rides again . . . Just a quick slice of—?'

'Afterwards,' she said, and wept as she said it. 'I'm sorry, I—'

He covered her mouth, then reached to the floor, retrieved his rifleman's helmet, put it on her head and loosened her robe. 'Get cracking, Private Wilton,' he said. 'I'm starving.'

They had dressed more formally than they usually did when they were alone, and she looked at the winding, twisting snake of lights and torches, cars, bicycles, carts, great crowds on foot, moving to the bonfire: God and sacrifice both.

They went to the table as Esteban appeared with the choicest wine they owned: wine so good she'd almost had to lie down and scream before he would open it. But, by the look of him, he too was on the cadge. He poured the wine. 'If I may ask, Señor Comandante,' he said.

'Nothing on God's earth is going to stop you,' said Callan.

'No, indeed, Señor Comandante. It concerns the yacht. It is very important, My Lady.'

'Yes,' she said. 'Yachts are always important. As soon as we've eaten.'

'Very good, My Lady.'

184

Esteban snapped his fingers and another manservant appeared, with cold tortillas. As Esteban served, Fiona went again to the balcony to watch the procession. Already the sky was dark, the lights glowed like jewels and the bonfire brooded like – like Moloch, would it be? The sky grew darker still.

At the end of the meal they drank Esteban's astonishing coffee.

'Did you get the idea Esteban's packed his bucket and spade already?' Callan asked.

'And his armbands,' she said. 'I suppose we'll see Roger and that luscious carnivore of his?'

'It's *his* yacht,' said Callan. 'Anyway, Esteban likes him. He'll let old Rog aboard.'

'So, it's jolly hols at last,' she said.

'Jolly Roger, too. Just one problem.'

'There's always a problem,' she said.

He took the photograph of Avram's chauffeur from an envelope, and a magazine clipping from *Ola!* Roger on the sun deck, happy, relaxed, in T-shirt and shorts, and Tiffany, equally happy and relaxed, in almost nothing. Serving them drinks was the chauffeur, this time a yacht steward. He passed the clippings to Fiona.

'Bishop?' she said.

'One of his merry murderers, more likely. You get the message?'

'Come here and talk money, or we'll kill your mate?'

He nodded.

'Suppose we don't go?'

'Pain, love. A hell of a lot of pain. For Roger. Tiffany too.'

'And if we do go . . . What chance would we have?'

'Chance?'

'To kill him,' she said. 'The chauffeur. Bishop, too. The whole stinking gang.'

'About as good as we'll ever get,' he said.

Her hand reached out: touched his. 'Then I don't see the problem,' she said, and then, excited as a little girl at the pantomime, 'Oh, look. They've started.'

185

He came to her, put his arm round her waist, and together they watched, as little jets of flame moved up the bonfire, busy, eager, until it gave its own light and the fireworks began, gleaming, thrusting, glowing like gold.

The bonfire was engulfed now, but fighting still, booming like artillery, throwing rockets at the sky. At its head, more fireworks preened like peacocks.

'He always did enjoy a good fire,' said Callan.

And he too glowed in the fire's light, she thought, and yet he's happy. Triumphant. Even though the whole night was red, his face, his body glowed, until there was nothing but the fire, menacing, magnificent, as if quite soon the world would begin. Or end.